The
Blind
Matriarch

ADVANCE PRAISE FOR THE BOOK

'In *The Blind Matriarch*, Namita Gokhale tackles our recent pandemic nightmare with courage and remarkable skill. It is a bold and entertaining novel by a hugely talented writer'—Chigozie Obioma

'Namita Gokhale is a master storyteller. Whenever I pick up her book, I always feel I am listening to her and not reading it. She has a rare art of tying up the time-ends in her narrative. That's what makes her stories classic. In *The Blind Matriarch*, she has stretched the experience of the two years of the pandemic to the entire middle-class behaviour of our times. Hats off to you, Namita!'—Gulzar

'Here is a profoundly Indian novel, a multi-layered narrative woven around an extended family, with a blind matriarch who holds it all together at its centre; her world, a universe of sounds and smells, vague shapes and sharp thoughts, that keep her alert to everything that goes on around her. The novel set in the context of the raging pandemic that turns everything upside-down is simultaneously a fascinating family story and a record of the gruesome days of the disease when dark death stalks the dreams of the living and tests their resilience and the solidity of their domestic and social bonds. Somewhere it also grows into an allegory of our existence as a nation with its vulnerabilities, its hierarchies, and its battles to transcend its losses and failures, touchingly narrated with all the confidence of a committed and experienced storyteller with her rare insights into human relationships with their complexities, and their special modes of surviving crises'—K. Satchidanandan

'Namita Gokhale's latest novel is a universal tale of love, loss, regret and stoicism in the year of the pandemic, where the acclaimed author of the searingly honest *Paro* now turns her attention to a joint family's sudden skirmish with mortality. Matangi Ma, the stoic, weather-beaten blind matriarch, presides over her large family, all living under one roof. She is a lady Dhritrashtra, with Lali, her long-suffering but loyal maid, reporting to her, Sanjaya-like, on family battles from ground zero. Matangi Ma has deep insights into what Death really is, even as her beloved grandchild describes his version of Death—a contemporary cross between Yama from Amar Chitra Katha and Thanos from *The Avengers*. The novel takes shape over a traumatic year and signals the end of an era. With its powerful meditations on both life and death, *The Blind Matriarch* is simultaneously Namita Gokhale's most sombre and life-affirming novel yet'—Mrinal Pande

The Blind Matriarch

NAMITA GOKHALE

PENGUIN
VIKING

An imprint of Penguin Random House

VIKING

USA | Canada | UK | Ireland | Australia
New Zealand | India | South Africa | China

Viking is part of the Penguin Random House group of companies
whose addresses can be found at global.penguinrandomhouse.com

Published by Penguin Random House India Pvt. Ltd
4th Floor, Capital Tower 1, MG Road,
Gurugram 122 002, Haryana, India

First published in Viking by Penguin Random House India 2021

10 9 8 7 6 5 4 3

ISBN 9780670093564

For sale in the Indian Subcontinent only

Typeset in Plantin MT Pro by Manipal Technologies Limited, Manipal
Printed at Thomson Press India Ltd, New Delhi

www.penguin.co.in

For we walk by faith, not by sight.

The present, the past. The dark, the light. Then and now. It was all blurred, in her heart, in her mind's eye.

Outside the window, on a branch of the old neem tree, the barbet was singing. Too-hay-too-hay. Too-hay-too-hay.

Was it just last year that they had found the bird, wounded, lying on the pavement below the red cotton tree? It looked defenceless, awkward; it had not quite learnt to fly. It had a large head, a long beak, green wings spattered with brown.

Lali had looked after the bird, helped it heal its wings. And then, one day, it had flown away.

She could hear Surya's deep voice, softly reading a poem aloud. He had not gone away, he was there still.

*'The past and the present wilt—I have fill'd them, emptied them
And proceed to fill my next fold of the future'*

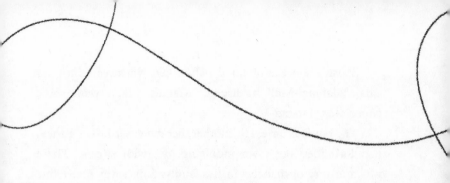

ONE

Her youngest grandson entered the room, shyly holding on to the curtain. She sensed his entry and called him to her, caressing the well-loved contours of his face. The skin soft as butter, the slightly oily hair, the hint of snot around his nose. She felt these things, inhaled them.

'Matangi-Ma!' he said. 'Matangi-Ma!'

She could imagine his face with her hands. The small nose. The large ears. Perhaps he looked like his father. Her sight had already begun failing when her youngest son was born.

Satish was born the day Sanjay Gandhi died. 23 June 1980. A harsh summer afternoon. She had already heard the news when she went into labour—thirty-three was no age to die.

It was a long and troubled labour. When at last she heard the baby cry, she smiled in relief through the tearing pain. Her lips were chapped and bitten and she could taste the salt of her tears.

She could not see his face clearly. It was a blur, even after she had wiped the tears. She strained to take it in, to remember and record his black eyes meeting hers, his rosebud mouth. Her son, Satish.

She had meant to name him Sanjay, but the plane crash had changed that. They decided to call him Satish, after her Mamaji, her mother's youngest brother.

Satish's son Rahul stood before her, whispering into her ears. 'Matangi-Ma!' he lisped, 'Matangi-Ma. I want some chocolate, Matangi-Ma.'

The boy was nine. His mother, her daughter-in-law Ritika, had forbidden her from indulging him with sweets. There was a history of diabetes in the family. Satish was borderline diabetic, and her Mamaji, also Satish, had been in a diabetic coma for nine months before he died.

'No chocolates, Matangi-Ma,' Ritika had said, just the day before. 'He is nine and already has two cavities.'

Ritika had complained to Satish as well, for that very evening her son had sat himself patiently beside her, not saying very much. She could sense from the hesitant way he cleared his throat that he was preparing to say something. It was only much later, after his cell phone rang, that he came out with it.

'Ritika is very upset, Matangi-Ma,' he said. 'Rahul is eating too much sugar. She found a bar of Cadbury chocolate under his pillow. It had half melted. He wouldn't say where he had got it from.'

He coughed. His phone rang again. He switched it off.

'I know . . . Ritika knows . . . how much you love Rahul. But we can't be blind to the damage you are doing him.'

He stopped. He had said the wrong thing. Nobody in the house ever spoke of her blindness. It was never mentioned, ever.

'Chocolate isn't good for children,' he said, retracing the conversation. 'Please, please, do this for me, for my sake, Ritika's sake. For the boy's sake. You must stop feeding him chocolate.'

And here he was, her Rahul, with cheeks like cooled butter, pleading for chocolate. She could try to imagine how his lips might have puckered up, how his eyebrows might rise and meet as his eyes met hers.

She could not refuse him anything. Anything. Ever.

She signalled to the maid, in the code they had evolved over the years. She tapped the wooden arm of the chair three times. Lali led the boy away, to the cupboard in the dressing room, to give him some toffees. They were easier to hide than the chocolate slabs, but sometimes the discarded wrappers gave them away.

Lali had come to her via her sister-in-law Sita, who lived in Nepalgunj. She had arrived when Matangi still had snatches of vision left. Lali was closer to her than anyone else in the world, and she retained a clear memory of what she looked like, or rather, what she had looked like.

Rahul was sucking at the toffee. Matangi stroked his face, imbibing the sweet caramel smell, wiping away the stickiness around his mouth.

'Tell me a story, Matangi-Ma.'

She didn't reply. She wanted to hear him say it again, and he did, in an insistent childish singsong voice, which evoked the telling of stories and the need for them to be told.

'Tell me a story, Matangi-Ma.'

She returned to the old story she had told and retold, for so many years, to so many generations of children and grandchildren.

'There were four young gods, immortals, who lived in the Himalayas. One day they heard the strains of human music, the sound of a flute playing . . .'

'What is a flute, Matangi-Ma?'

'What Lord Krishna plays—a bamboo pipe. I can't believe you are such a silly, little Rahul!'

Lali pointed to the gold-framed picture of Lord Krishna that hung on the wall and pretended to play on an imaginary flute. Her fingers were spread out against her mouth and there was a beatific expression on her broad face. She let out a low flute-like sound from her throat.

Rahul observed her warily. Matangi could sense Lali's movement; she could guess what she was doing.

'Stop these silly sounds, Lali!' she commanded, and drew Rahul close to her again. She inhaled the scent of hair oil and his toffee breath. Her heart expanded with love.

Ritika entered the room, smelling of garlic. Her high heels clicked on the mosaic floor. 'Time to do your homework, Rahul,' she said in an expressionless voice. 'You shouldn't trouble your grandmother all the time.'

Matangi wondered, as she often did, about the colour of Ritika's eyes. Were they brown? Black? She had never held her close, stroked her face, understood its contours. She scarcely knew her, except as a voice and a clattering of heels that arrived to take Rahul away.

The scent of garlic was overlaid with the scent of roses. Talcum powder, she concluded.

'What have you been cooking, Ritika?' Matangi asked gently.

'Chicken,' Ritika replied, an edge of defiance to her voice. 'A French recipe. For Rahul and his father. In my kitchen.'

The four-storeyed house had been designed by an apprentice to Lawrence Wilfred 'Lawrie' Baker, the British-born Indian architect, and mimicked his distinctive style. The red brick screens provided shade and ventilation, and the different levels led into each other through a gently curved stairway that was effectively a spine to the architectural plan. Each floor was completely independent of the others, and yet they were integrally connected and held together by the airy 'jali' walls, and the mellow light they filtered in.

Matangi's daughter Shanta lived on the ground floor, which was fronted by a small garden. She was a little mother to the whole family and cooked for her siblings at every opportunity. Matangi's meals, and Lali's, were sent up from Shanta's kitchen in a tiffin carrier. Matangi was strictly vegetarian, and Shanta's maid, Munni, ladled out tureens of perfectly consistent dal, fragrant rice and the vegetables of the season—cabbage, cauliflower, tinda, lauki, spinach. Her fabled biryani was reserved for Suryaveer on the first floor.

Munni came in to collect the empty lunchbox, carrying a plate of besan laddoos with her. Rahul was led out, whining slightly. Lali shut the door after them, and made an expressive sound, indicating disapproval. She didn't like Ritika and gossiped about her endlessly.

Matangi retreated into herself. 'Leave me alone, Lali,' she said. 'I'm not in the mood for idle chatter.'

She was weary and needed to sleep. Rahul had arrived at the time of her afternoon nap. Although she could no longer keep time according to the movement of daylight and night darkness, her body had not forgotten the sure rhythm of the passing hours.

Ritika had brought her a cuckoo clock from Switzerland, after their honeymoon. It had hung on the alcove behind the window for ten years now, softly announcing the time every hour and half hour. CUCKOO. CUCKOO. CUCKOO. CUCKOO. It was four o'clock.

'I want to sleep,' she told Lali. She reached for the handkerchief under her pillow, tracing the pattern of embroidered flowers with her fingers.

Matangi's mother had given her an embroidery kit and a book on the 'how-tos' of various styles of embroidery—basic cross-stitch, beautiful French knots, even detailed needlepoint. As a teenager, she had spent long hours embroidering twelve cambric handkerchiefs, intended as a part of her wedding trousseau. She had dreamt of how her husband would delight in and compliment her artistry, the flowers and birds she conjured up with needle and thread. Perhaps she would make special ones for him, monogrammed with his name.

Three of the handkerchiefs had miraculously survived— they had remained her companions through those years of pain and torture, consoling her, wiping her tears. Shanta had bought her new ones as well, from a silai school that she supported, which trained young girls in the crafts. Matangi smoothed out the handkerchief and put it away.

'Wake me up at five,' she continued. 'Not ginger tea, I want masala tea.'

She rarely dreamed in the afternoon, but today some confused images were dredged up from the past. She was in a hospital bed, her legs splayed apart, singing a song. A clock hung on the wall before her, a round orb like a sun or a moon. A plane crashed to earth from somewhere in the sky. The clock became a bird which swooped around the room. CUCKOO, CUCKOO, CUCKOO, CUCKOO, CUCKOO, it announced, before it flew out of the open window. Then the dream ceased, vanished, and she was sweating slightly under her Rajasthani quilt as Lali brought her tea and biscuits.

Lali handed her the dentures she had placed in a steel tumbler while Matangi napped. The tea revived her, with the flavours of cardamom and cinnamon rippling through her body like a tide. She attempted to dunk a biscuit in the tea, only to have it land on her arm with a soft splat.

'Toothless, and blind,' she said aloud, with an ironic smile.

'What did you say, Mataji?' Lali asked as she wiped the tea-soaked biscuit off her arm.

'Nothing,' she murmured. 'Nothing at all. I want some more tea, that's all.'

Matangi had discovered, quite by accident, that if she pressed on the roof of her mouth, she could centre and correlate her sharpened senses better. This had become a private ritual to orient herself, to find her way through the grainy darkness. She rolled her tongue against her palate, exploring its contours. It cleared the mist sometimes and helped her balance herself. She felt as though she had eyes everywhere, in her fingertips, in her silver be-ringed toes, in the alert grey hairs that stood up on end on her thin arms, and her elbows, even.

Lali went out, past the veranda and the corridor, to the small kitchen on the third floor, to prepare the tea. Matangi could hear someone whining outside, a soft sound suspended between a human and animal scale. A child? A dog? It was not a cat.

Lali brought in the tea, but it didn't taste as good this second time. It was too hot, and it scalded her mouth. There was ginger in it, too much ginger.

'What is that sound?' she asked sharply. 'That sound from outside, from the veranda.'

'It is my nephew,' Lali replied. There was a defensive note in her voice, an attempt at appeasement. 'My sister's son. Jijaji left him here today. My sister died last year—you know that. The father has gone to Kathmandu for a carpentry contract. I didn't know what else to do with him. I've told him to sit quietly in the veranda. But children will be children. They will laugh, they will cry. They will play.'

Matangi looked around her sightlessly. She could hear the child, but not sense him. 'Let him be,' she said, suddenly tired. 'But just for a day. Or two.'

She needed to nap again. Lali covered her up gently with the floral Rajasthani quilt, and listened attentively to her rhythmic snoring before she tiptoed out of the room.

In the veranda, the child was asleep too, curled up on the cement floor next to the pots of mogra and raat-ki-rani. The late-afternoon sun cast its dappled light upon him. A tiny ant crawled across his arm.

Lali looked out of the balcony at the scene below. Three drivers were clustered around the gate, gossiping. An auto-rickshaw stopped to ask them for directions. Little Rahul peered out of the gate curiously.

Matangi descended into sleep again, where she was accosted by unfamiliar colours. The orange of some forgotten sunset seemed to have soaked into her retina. She could hear her eldest son Suryaveer reciting a poem by Dinkar that he had learnt in school. It was from *Rashmirathi*.

Varshon tak van mein ghoom ghoom
Badha-vighnon ko choom choom
Saubhagya na sab din sota hai
Dekho, aage kya hota hai?

Suryaveer's gravelly voice repeated the lines again and again, like a stuck record. She could still remember them when she awoke.

What recesses of memory had that come from, she wondered. The exiled Pandavas' wanderings in the forest, and their acceptance of misfortune, followed by the assertion, or at least the tentative hope, that good fortune would not remain asleep for ever.

Dekho, aage kya hota hai? It was like the beginning of a novel or a television serial. *Let's see what happens next?*

She enjoyed television serials. After her midday nap, Matangi could often be found tuning into the repeats of old soap operas with Lali by her side as she listened to the unfolding drama. Her favourite was, always had been, and would remain *Kyonki Saas Bhi Kabhi Bahu Thi*. She could not view them, but Matangi knew and recognized each of the characters from their voices. She fancied herself as Ba, the wise and beloved matriarch of a large extended family. As indeed she was.

Then that girl Tulsi had to spoil it all. She went back to being Smriti Irani. She was an important political leader now, minister-shinister and all that. The new serials didn't have the same flavour; they simply didn't reach out to Matangi in the same way.

It was only the other day that she heard Tulsi's voice on television. She recognized it instantly. 'That's Tulsi!' she told Lali excitedly. 'That's my Tulsi!'

'No, Mataji, that's not Tulsi. You are talking of an imaginary character. This is Smriti Irani. Member of Parliament. Minister. She defeated Rahul Gandhi in the last election, from Amethi.'

Tulsi had been speaking of Rahul Gandhi, who she referred to sarcastically as Shehenshah. But Matangi was not interested in Smriti Irani—only in Tulsi. She had told Lali to switch the television off.

Saubhagya na sab din sota hai
Dekho, aage kya hota hai?

Good fortune does not forever slumber
Let's see what happens next?

Well, she could certainly not *see* what lay ahead, though she could imagine it. Misfortune had followed Matangi all her life. She had been ten when her father died. Her papa, DCP Matang Singh Kashyap, of the newly independent Indian Police Service, had been posted in Assam. They had been in Dibrugarh when the earthquake struck.

It was 15 August. Independence Day. She had gone with her parents for the flag-hoisting ceremony; she had watched the Tiranga unfurl, observed the rose petals flutter out of it and fall to the ground. She detected tears welling up in her mother's smiling eyes. Independent India was three years old. Matangi had been enthralled by it all and gorged on the sweet and savoury pitha, and the egg shoaps, that were served up afterwards.

Later, before the earthquake, she had a stomach ache from eating too much. It was raining, just a drizzle really. The sun had long set, and the curtains were drawn. The clock on the wall said 7.40 p.m. She was still wearing her best clothes, the frilly orange frock and striped socks. Her mother had forbidden her from taking her socks off. She could not, until this day, aged eighty, ever forget how the ground had begun shaking. The dangling light bulb was jerking this way and that, like a temple bell, and the wooden floor planks were jumping about, like keys in a piano.

'Don't move, Matangi!' she could hear her mother scream. 'Don't move! I am coming to get you.'

There was a sound of ululation all around—trees howling, wooden rafters wailing, the earth weeping. A lizard had tumbled from its perch on the wall and fallen on her shoulders. Her mother had rushed her out, and they were in the veranda, when the tree fell. She had never forgotten the darkness that had overtaken them. The roar of the earth splitting apart drowned out all but the faint crackle of the wires snapping. Her mother had left her out alone in the dark. She could hear the cows mooing. There were only blurred memories after that, of her father, dead, and the changes that were to follow. 15 August 1950. Independence Day.

The smell of oranges. The sharp, tender sweet fragrance of narangi. Matangi inhaled it and was lulled and distracted. Who was eating oranges?

'Lali!' she called sharply. 'Lali!' There was no reply.

Matangi liked to peel oranges. The texture of the rind would remain in her fingers, and the scent would make her smile.

Where was Lali?

Lali was outside in the veranda, with the child. What was she to do with him?

The Blind Matriarch

She had fed him a besan laddoo and shared an orange with him. He looked lost and disinterested. 'Come into the room with me,' she said. 'Let's watch television.'

Inside, the old woman was still going on about oranges.

'I ate an orange, Mataji,' she responded patiently. 'I was feeling a little sick, and I knew you wouldn't mind.' Matangi grunted. 'The orange was sour, anyway!' Lali added inconsequentially.

'Switch on the television,' Matangi commanded. 'I want to hear the news. It's important to know what's going on in the world.'

'Which channel do you want to watch, Mataji?' Lali asked, a shake of impatience in her voice. 'English or Hindi? Doordarshan, NDTV, or ZEE?'

Matangi made no reply. Lali checked the channels, playing around with the remote, instructing the boy through stern gestures to remain silent.

'Doordarshan,' Matangi declared. 'I want to listen to Doordarshan.'

The boy sat cross-legged before the television set and looked blankly at the screen before him.

The news. A riot. A bye-election. The China virus.

'Turn it off, Lali,' Matangi said wearily. 'I don't want to hear the news.'

Lali complied. She turned the sound off, and continued to switch channels until she located a Japanese cartoon network. She motioned to the child and indicated with her hands and eyes that he should watch. Then she frowned, raised her eyebrows and put her finger to her lips, signalling with her hands that she would spank him if he spoke or made a sound.

The child watched warily, trying to make sense of the figures on the screen. Slowly, the story, or what he could make of it, drew him in, and he watched with delight and anticipation as the strange creatures chased each other through a flattened landscape of rainbow colours.

He couldn't help but let out a little gasp of joy. Matangi heard him, and smiled, as though unsurprised.

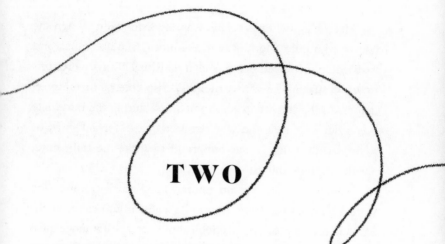

TWO

On the floor below, a candlelit dinner.

Ritika had put the lights off, though the streetlights cast neon shadows from the windows and the halogen in the kitchen and the LED in the corridor had, of course, been left on.

Satish didn't appreciate wine, so they were drinking beer instead. Normal glasses, not beer tankards, although they had a set of six in the wood and bevelled-glass cupboard that showcased their crockery. Kingfisher Lite, as Satish didn't appreciate that expensive stuff in cans, either.

The chicken hadn't come out quite as she had expected; it was rubbery and chewy and frankly unappetizing. But they were doing fine with the garlic bread. Satish liked garlic. And onions. And mint.

'Let's try a tandoori chicken next time,' he ventured cautiously.

'Well, you could try making it next time for a change, Mr Satish!' she replied in a tone that teetered between the flirtatious and the shrewish. 'We both have jobs, we both enjoy food, so perhaps you could develop your cooking talents too!'

The candle flickered. The lipstick had snagged on her lips.

He kissed her tenderly on her cheek. 'I will make you a tandoori chicken,' he promised. 'Next week.'

Her job in the travel agency was not taxing even though she had to commute a long way to the office. She was quick and focused, and enjoyed being in charge. Ritika always wore saris to work; silks in the winter months, crisp cottons in summer, nylons during the monsoon. Sometimes, during the rains, she broke her own rule and wore trousers and a formal shirt, or a kurta with jeans. It was important to strike the right note, always, in these things.

Today at home, to commemorate the 'French evening', she wore a diaphanous dress—not quite a gown but near enough. She had read a post on Facebook about keeping romance alive and had decided to give it a shot.

It had been an arranged marriage, even though they had met a few times before they finally made up their minds. Satish had been a romantic at heart—he still was. He held her hand, examining the lines on her palm, which couldn't possibly be visible in the dim candlelight. She stroked his arm in response, feeling the soft underside, the rough knuckles, the wiry hairs around his wrist.

'What can you see in the dark?' she asked teasingly. An image flashed in her mind, of her mother-in-law in the room upstairs, bathed in perpetual darkness. She tried to change the subject, but Satish had already picked up the thread.

'I know every line of your palm,' Satish replied. 'I know every frown and wrinkle and laugh-line of your face. Even in the dark.'

Something in her mood had changed. She was still thinking of her blind mother-in-law. She shuddered.

'Your mother . . .' Ritika said. 'Your mother can see in the dark too. Sometimes I think she is not really blind; maybe she sees everything and we don't realize it.' She had the sense to control herself, to hold herself back. 'Matangi-Ma is really courageous,' she continued insincerely. 'I really admire her for how she carries on, despite her handicap.'

Ritika's smile drooped as she made her way to the kitchen. Their maid, Irina, who lived in the slum cluster nearby usually stayed on to do the dishes, but there was a no-show today. 'Kaf and Fiver,' she had reported in the WhatsApp message. Ritika had correctly decrypted her message. 'Cough and fever'. Irina was twelfth-pass and proficient in Hindi; it was her ambition to be fluent in English as well.

One had to be careful with coughs and fevers, what with the coronavirus spreading out of Wuhan. She would have to wash the dishes herself today. After her manicure yesterday— how annoying! But at least there was no residue of oil and turmeric and spices to foul up the plates after a continental-cuisine meal, she consoled herself.

Rahul was in his room, hopefully asleep. Satish had gone for a walk. Ritika settled herself on the cane chair in the narrow balcony and lit up a cigarette. Holi was approaching but the air was still cool. The waxing moon was playing hide-and-seek between the branches of the neem tree. The scent of fragrant night flowers descended from Matangi's veranda. Everything about the evening was sensuous and seductive. She stretched herself and admired the pleated flounces of her diaphanous dress. She sighed and examined her nails. This sense of yearning that consumed her—what was it?

Her hands smelt of garlic. The beer was making her fart. She felt bloated. Ritika puffed on her cigarette and thought of Paris. They had gone to France and Switzerland for their honeymoon. Satish had kissed her on the lips, out there in front of everybody. They had ascended the Eiffel Tower and contemplated the Matterhorn.

A strange sound descended from the floor above, from Mataji's veranda. Somewhere between a wailing, a keening and a serenade, it played with the rapturous scents of the night flowers, with the jasmine and the raat-ki-rani.

She could make out the words now, even though the tune was unrecognizable. It was her mother-in-law, singing to the moon she could not see. Like a dog, or a lunatic.

Ritika stubbed out her cigarette, then realized she needn't have. The old lady was blind as a bat. She wouldn't know the giveaway gleam of the lit cigarette, even if she sensed the cigarette smoke. Damn. She shouldn't have stubbed it out. Damn.

She lit up another cigarette. She hadn't given an undertaking not to smoke, had she, when she got married? In a joint family, everybody had to adjust. Everybody.

She strained to listen to the words. *Jaane kahaan gaye woh din*. That was the song her mother-in-law was singing. There was a pleasing quality to her voice, Ritika reflected, even though the pitch was too low.

The singing stopped. She heard a long sigh, then silence.

Had Matangi-Ma smelt the cigarette smoke? Probably not, she concluded. There were too many contending aromas. The exhaust fan from the downstairs kitchen wafted up the fragrance of spiced freshly cooked rice. A passing van spewed diesel fumes. This was a city of many scents, many smells.

She inhaled the fragrance of the night flowers and smiled. The moon behind the neem tree emerged to smile back at her.

Lali helped Mataji walk back to the room. She didn't usually need a walker or a stick, but today she had refused Lali's arm and used the aluminium walker to tread her cautious way to the balcony. TAK TAK TAK TAK!

It was time to pick up the dinner from Shanta-didi. Lali set off downstairs on her daily chore, smiling to herself as she walked down the steps of the central staircase. She had seen Ritika smoking in her balcony and added it to the record of secrets that she carried around in her head, like a hidden bank account.

The first-floor flat was still locked up. Suryaveer-sahib and Samir bhaiyya were travelling to Simla. They had left the keys with Shanta-didi in the ground floor. Their dog, Dollar, was parked with Shanta as well. The door was open when Shanta went to pick up the dinner tiffin, and she received a rapturous welcome from him.

The large steel-and-plastic tiffin carrier was waiting on the kitchen table. 'What took you so long?' Shanta chided. 'Ma must be hungry!'

'Mataji was in a romantic mood,' she replied, 'singing a filmi geet for the moon, and so I got late. Poor Ritika memsahib had to stub out her cigarette on the balcony below us.' She doubled over, giggling to herself, but her eyes were on Shanta, gauging her reactions.

Shanta was, as her name suggested, a calm person, not given to being entertained by staff gossip. She raised an eyebrow, as much reproof as question, and pointed to the kitchen table.

Lali returned to the top floor to find Matangi seated on a chair, stroking the child's face.

'See that he eats properly,' Matangi said. 'He feels thin and hungry.'

They slept huddled together that night, Lali and the child, in the curtained-off corner of the veranda that served as her bedroom.

Shanta was watching television with her cat, a large ginger with an amused expression and a remarkably bushy tail. She was avoiding the news channels, trying to blank out images of charred homes and toxic hatred. It was that or the Chinese virus—very little else seemed to be occupying the minds of the media.

Shanta had spent two harrowing days in northeast Delhi with colleagues from her organization. The encounters with women who had lost almost everything and who still summoned up the courage to carry on with their lives had scarred her at a personal level in a way nothing had ever done before. Caste, community and religion seemed all that remained in the debris of life. She couldn't believe that the India she thought she knew had changed so much. Or perhaps it had always been like this.

Thank God the Trump visit was over, although the Melania–Taj Mahal memes were still surfacing. It amused her that her cat was named Trump, and that they were watching the news together. Trump was a lady, biologically and by temperament. Ah well, the world would go on, she told herself philosophically—cats and presidents, goons and vandals, liberals and fascists, fashionistas and feminists. They were all in it together, and they would all just have to carry on.

A dog named Dollar and a cat named Trump. It was amusing in a cheesy sort of way. She had no idea where or why her brother Suryaveer and his adopted son had picked up a thin, anxious stray and decided to call him Dollar. There must be a complicated reason for it, a backstory. It was a given that nothing about Surya was ever simple.

His switch from left-wing commitment to right-wing obfuscation had not taken her by surprise. Shanta had observed her kind, compassionate elder brother and his constant ideological struggles since she was a teenager. Suryaveer had been a vegetarian, a pacifist, an anarchist, a Marxist Leninist, a Gandhian, and now veered to the soft right, lurching from conviction to conviction in a sequence of seemingly reasoned responses.

Although he was no longer a vegetarian, she felt he had settled down now to the emotional territory and belief system that might be expected of an upper-caste Brahmin of a certain age. His friends from all the various stages of his life continued to remain devoted to him and overlooked his turnarounds with cautious indulgence.

Suryaveer was extremely fond of his pragmatic sister Shanta and counted on her to mediate the frequent confusions in his life. She loved him unconditionally, and knew she could count on him always, which was more than could be said of her other sibling Satish.

Shanta was playing with Trump and listening to the news when the doorbell rang. There were three policemen waiting outside, two men and a woman officer. They asked if they could come in. Shanta settled them at her dining table and sat down patiently before them. Years of NGO work had taught her how to handle the police.

She told Munni to get some water, asked them if they would have some tea. The plump, capable-looking lady cop asked for coffee. She seemed puzzled by the French press contraption that Munni produced, but negotiated her way through it with admirable poise.

'Myself Babli Mohan,' she said pleasantly. 'And my colleagues Shri Kirpa Ram and Kundan Singh-ji.' The policemen shifted their bodies in acknowledgement and made eye contact with each other.

'There has been a police complaint about your neighbours,' she said. 'C102, next door. Do you know them, madam? When did you last meet them?'

C102. Agastya Sen was a retired diplomat. He had been the Indian ambassador to Poland. His wife Anna was Eastern European, possibly Hungarian. She had last seen them more than two months ago. They had been taking a walk on Christmas day. She remembered because she had wished them a merry Christmas. Anna had sent over some cake later that evening.

'Any other information?' Babli Mohan asked crisply. 'You see, they have gone missing. Their domestic staff called the police and raised an alarm. There is no evidence of theft or foul play. Yet.'

Shanta knew better than to tangle with policemen—police persons—looking to close a case. She did not volunteer any further information. 'That's all I know,' she said and gave Babli her card.

'Please keep me in the picture. I am naturally very concerned about our neighbours. They seemed very nice people, from the little I knew of them.'

'Shanta Sharma.' Babli Mohan read out the details of her card almost accusingly. 'Women for Peace.' So, you are a NGO wallah? Shaheen Bagh? JNU type? Urban Naxals? Terrorism. Sedition. Best to be careful, madam, in these days. I know you are a good lady, and you mean well, but . . .'

She scribbled her name on a piece of paper torn from her notepad, along with her mobile number. 'Always there to help you, Miss Shanta, if you need me. And please inform if you get any information on your neighbours, on Mr and Mrs Sen.'

The two policemen had not spoken a word. They left together, joining their palms in polite namastes before they marched out.

The encounter had tired Shanta. She had been meaning to visit her mother, but she was suddenly too wearied and fatigued. Munni was hovering around, curiosity writ large on her face. Shanta was in no mood to engage with her.

'Get me some chamomile tea, Munni,' she commanded. 'I don't want your chatter, please. Any gossip or information can wait until tomorrow.'

She switched on the television, searching for a channel that was not obsessing about the coronavirus. Elsewhere, the Madhya Pradesh government was facing a challenge. Legislators were being held hostage. 'Political drama is always entertaining,' she told herself, 'and also instructive.' But five minutes into the news she tuned out and switched the television off.

Matangi prepared to go to sleep. It was never easy. The end of the day did not bring a sense of exhaustion; instead, she would feel more awake, more alive, as the evening set in. She had relished the meal that Shanta had sent her. The dal, the potatoes and the peas pulao, served at the small table by the wall. She waited for her daughter to come up, as she usually did. She instructed Lali to feed the child properly. And then, as the cuckoo clock sang out the time, she went and lay down resignedly on her bed.

Ten o'clock was shutdown time. Lali would return to the veranda to FaceTime and talk on the phone with her family. She would lie awake listening to the street sounds, the barking dogs, sometimes the hoot of an owl from somewhere in the park.

The scent of the night flowers had crept into her room. Jasmine. Mogra. Raat-ki-rani. She breathed them in and smiled in the dark. The waking dreams that made up the long nights began to enfold her.

She was about to drift into half-sleep when her cell phone vibrated. It was her daughter, Shanta. Nobody else ever called her. Matangi held the old Blackberry close to her ear. She loved the sound of her daughter's voice. It was calm, like her name, and musical.

'Are you well, Mummy?' Shanta asked. 'Sorry I couldn't come up today, too many things happened. Will be there tomorrow, with your breakfast. I'm making idli with coconut chutney. Goodnight, darling Mummy. Keep me in your prayers.'

Her prayers! Did her children assume that Matangi-Ma was a deeply religious person? Well, she wasn't a disbeliever or an atheist, certainly not; but she had a contentious relationship with the gods. They had been unjust with her, and she was unforgiving in her anger and her disappointment.

Only the goddess was spared her anger; only Matangi, whom she was named after. She had stopped praying to

Matangi, stopped asking for her boons, but sometimes, in her dreams, the goddess appeared to her. On those nights, she could sense her, Uchchhishta-Matangini, with her sword, her club, her goad and her noose. A parrot hovered around her, joyous and keen-eyed.

Matangi returned to her dream memories, lulled by the night flowers. She conjured up the moon, and the touch of times past—of children sleeping on her bed, of pressing her husband's bony feet, of kneading flour to make chapatis on the griddle. Of his forbidden lips, his gentle arms. All these were gathered up into a single wave of longing, to be held, to be touched.

When at last she fell asleep, she was clutching her handkerchief, feeling and stroking the border of roses and petals, investing it with her memories and longings. She awoke to Lali's giggles and whispered phone conversation. The cuckoo clock chimed reprovingly. Another day. One more morning, afternoon, evening to be negotiated.

She pushed back her hair from her eyes and smiled. 'Good morning, Lali,' she said cheerfully.

'Good morning, Mataji!' Lali replied. 'Good morning.'

And then the child, in a warm, woolly voice, 'Good morning, Mataji.' The patter of little feet, his arms around her. 'Good morning, Mataji.'

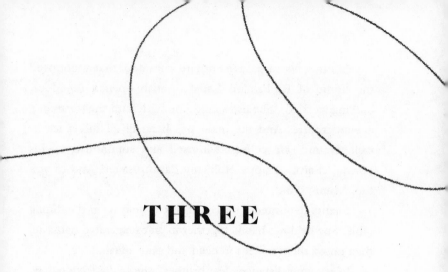

THREE

It's Holi. 10 March. The festival of colours is meant to usher in the onset of summer, but not this year. It's cold and windy and cloudy. The Holika fire the night before whimpered in the breeze. The coronavirus is keeping people indoors, and the prime minister has urged people to celebrate the rowdy festival with the utmost restraint.

On the ground floor of C100, Shanta has been cooking up a storm. She has baked two batches of gujiyas, made with organic flour and suji, and coated them in a gentle cardamom-flavoured syrup. Munni, among her many roles that of an accomplished cook, wanted to fry them, but Shanta wanted them baked. It was a new recipe, and once the gujiyas had been coated with a patina of silver virk, Shanta placed them in four baskets, along with a sprig of larkspur from her tiny garden, with its first blooms of spring.

No colours this year, not even dry, powdered ones. Nobody trusted the Chinese imports any more, and the fear of the virus had led her, like most of her friends, to be cautious.

Dollar the dog and Trump the cat were left behind as the two women set off on their festive excursion. Munni rang the bell on the first floor and tried to peep in from the eyehole. Shanta tried to call her brother but he seemed to be out of range.

Another floor up, to the ornate front door that announced the home of Ritika and Satish. Satish opened the door, looking worried. 'She has a cold,' he said, 'and she is running a temperature. And the maid has been ill all this week as well. Damn!' He collected himself and summoned up his normal charm. 'Happy Holi, my darling sister! And to you too, Munni didi.'

Shanta deposited a basket of baked gujiyas on the dining table. She held her hands together in an exaggerated namaste, then raised them to her forehead and said Adaab.

'Keep your distance, dear brother,' she said affectionately. 'And a very happy Holi to all of you. I must rush up to see Mummy now, I never got to visit her last evening, what with the police coming in.'

Satish's even-featured face betrayed no curiosity. 'The police?' he asked softly. 'What have you been up to, sis?'

'It can wait,' Shanta replied as she rushed up the stairs. 'Will catch up later.'

Matangi was sitting on her bed, her hands spread out before her, as though she were examining her nail polish. Her mother's blindness had been an ingrained part of Shanta's life since she was young. The macular degeneration and retinopathy that led to her loss of vision was a factual reality to Matangi's children. Her own unflustered acceptance of her condition had made it all seem even more normal.

Because the retinal damage had set in gradually, Matangi had adapted her faculties to the blurred vision. She went about her tasks with easy, relaxed movements, never complaining, never letting on how little she could actually see. She had not even noticed when and how her instincts had begun to take over, and when her sense of hearing, of smell, even of taste, had become sharper, more acute. Her fingertips, her toes, even the hairs on her arm, were all part of the apparatus of perception.

The Blind Matriarch

'Admiring your nail polish, are you?' Shanta asked. They joked a lot together, and her mother's sly humour still had the capacity to catch her daughter unawares.

'What to do? *Tu ne mehndi lagane nahin di*!' Matangi responded, an affectionate smile lighting up her face. Her daughter's determined spinsterhood had not disappointed her. In fact, she endorsed the independence that came with Shanta's single life. Yet it surprised and puzzled her that only one of her three children had ever taken the plunge. She would have liked to imagine Surya and Shanta married and settled, rather than treading the uncharted trajectories they had chosen.

Munni had unwrapped the baked gujiyas and put them on a plate. She offered them to Lali and the child, who seemed in a state of high excitement. Shanta put a speck of colour on her mother's lined forehead and respectfully bent down to touch her feet. Her beautiful feet, which seemed to stay young even as the rest of her body aged.

'What's your name, beta?' she asked the child.

'Riyaz,' he replied, 'But Lali aunty has asked me to say it is Pappoo.'

There was a moment of silence, as they took that in, all in their different ways. Lali's face was inscrutable. Shanta took control, as always.

'Well then I suppose it's Pappoo,' she said brightly but with firm emphasis. 'Lali is always right! Glad to meet you, Pappoo, and wishing you a very happy Holi.'

Matangi was humming a Holi thumri. Her voice was wheezy today, but tuneful.

'*Udit abeer gulal*,' she sang wistfully, almost as though she could see the greens and reds and pinks of the colours flung in the air. 'I have heard Girija Devi singing it, years ago, when . . .'

Matangi never mentioned the past except in terms of 'when.'

'It's Raag Mishra Gara,' she continued composedly. 'Let's switch on some Holi music since nobody is celebrating in any other way.'

But Lali was in the mood for gossip. 'I heard the police came to you yesterday, Shanta didi,' she exclaimed, the excitement and curiosity palpable on her face. 'Old Mr Sen and his phoren wife have disappeared? Their sweeper thinks they have run away because of corona-shorona. Maybe they are murdered? Or suicided?'

A burst of laughter came in from the front door, and Suryaveer and Samir tumbled into the room. 'Holi Mubarak, Matangi-Ma!' they shouted, as they flung a shower of rose petals over her.

Matangi's face was suffused with joy. Her firstborn was the most beloved of her three children. 'Where had you disappeared, Surya?' she asked him tenderly. 'You left for Simla without even meeting me.'

Suryaveer gave a complicated reply, which involved an unexpected field trip, an old friend and a hailstorm. He had a way of wandering off the main point, which could be both charming and infuriating, depending on the circumstances.

Matangi was caressing the skin of the rose petals strewn around her. She would stroke them as though she could sense each petal, speak to it. She inhaled deeply, and a beatific smile settled on her face.

The child wanted another gujiya. 'And who is this young gent?' Surya asked, chucking him under his cheek as he spoke.

'My nephew Pappoo,' Lali replied quickly. 'Only for a few days staying with me, Surya sir.'

Samir had been silent all this time, preoccupied with his phone. 'I have to rush,' he murmured and scooted off downstairs. Suryaveer followed in his wake.

Shanta and her mother sat quietly together, taking in this unusually hushed Holi, stripped of all festivity.

Both of them, separately, were remembering another Holi, almost thirty-five years ago. They had lived in Kaka Nagar then, in a cramped government flat. The three children shared a small bedroom, which led into another bedroom, occupied by their parents.

Their father was working in the defence ministry, in the department of audits and accounts. He had a toothbrush moustache, which made him look like Hitler or Charlie Chaplin or Asrani in *Sholay*, depending on the viewer's perspective.

They had received a lot of gifts that Holi—a carton of jams, laddoos, gujiyas, even a silver platter with colours in it. There was a Holi party in the park outside; Shanta could still remember the swirl of colours, yellow, red, green, red, and the laughing faces all around her.

Later, she had waited patiently to use the bathroom, to scrub the pucca colour off her face and arms. Satish had bathed already, although there was a streak of purple across his nose which had refused to come off. Surya was taking forever in the bathroom, and she was worried there would be no water left for her by the time he finished.

Her father hadn't bathed yet. Neither had her mother. They had been arguing in their bedroom. She had never heard her mother raise her voice before, never to *him*, but she was speaking louder than she usually did, and more forcefully. From the sound of her voice, Shanta decided that she had been weeping as well.

Shanta had peeped cautiously through the drawn curtains. Her father was slapping her mother; she could hear the sound of his palm as it settled on her cheeks. Once, twice, thrice. The slaps reverberated across her colour-drenched cheeks. Then he pulled at her hair, at the long plait, so that her neck jerked backwards and her eyes rolled around in their orbs. Another resounding slap, and then he went inside their bathroom to bathe.

Her mother didn't see Shanta. Her vision had begun to fail already, and her daughter had positioned herself deep in the folds of the handloom curtains. She sat down on the bed with her head in her hands. She didn't weep.

The evening that followed was like any other. Her mother had cooked chhole chawal. The excitement of the festival had left them all ravenous. After dinner they gorged on the sweets, the laddoos and gujiyas, that had arrived as Holi gifts for their father.

Suryaveer had a bad stomach and kept going to the toilet all night. She slept next to him on an adjoining bed, while Satish slept on the diwan against the wall, under the window which was always shut.

Shanta worried about her mother all night and resolved to confront her father the next morning. But he left early for office, and her mother seemed quite normal and composed. What could she say or do?

She never forgot that scene, and every now and then, during Holi, it rose with a tide of tormented childhood memories.

Munni and Lali were still chattering in the balcony. The boy was staring at them with his big eyes. It was silent outside— no excited screeches, no rubber balloons being hurled at strangers. This Holi. That Holi. Shanta had cooked chhole chawal for lunch. 'Bring Mataji her food, once you are finished gossiping!' she told Munni. 'Or tell Lali to come down and get it.'

'I'm not hungry,' Matangi said. 'I will just have an orange or a banana, I think.'

'I've made you chhole chawal, Mummy,' Shanta insisted.

'I will have it for dinner,' Matangi said wearily. She lay down on her bed, her face to the wall.

She too remembered that Holi. She had seen him with that woman, watched them go into the house together. Matangi had been in her forties. Her vision had begun to blur, her long curly hair gone grey at the temples. She washed her face with Lux soap. Lacto Calamine in the daytime, Ponds cold cream at night. Cuticura talc. Keo Karpin hair oil. A hint of kajal around her eyes sometimes. Two Lakmé lipsticks. She had never been beautiful, but she was a dutiful wife, a good mother. She never wasted his money.

He had slapped her that Holi. Not for the first time. Not the last. She had packed her clothes that night; three saris, underwear and a towel in the old attaché case he took on his official tours. She packed her embroidered handkerchiefs, the remnants of her long-ago dreams. She would not leave them behind. She would walk away, run away, escape. She would sit in the railway station, all night, in the ladies waiting room, and then take whatever train left in the morning. Anywhere. Etawah. Visakhapatnam. Places where she knew nobody, where nobody knew her.

But she didn't leave. Of course, she could not leave. She had resigned herself to being a prisoner in that house, in that life. She was an Indian woman, a Hindu lady. She had children. She had nowhere to go.

Her vision began to blur even more. She had chosen not to see. Perhaps she had resolved to become blind.

Her husband, Prabodh Kumar Sharma, of the Indian audits and accounts service. He had loved pakodas and chhole puri. And other people's wives.

That house. That life. It was all so long ago that she scarcely remembered it. She was secure in this quiet dimness, with her children around her.

'Get me a gujiya, Lali,' she said. 'And an orange as well.'

Later in the afternoon, Rahul wandered up to visit her.

'My mother is not well,' he explained gravely, 'and my papa has a headache as well. I wasn't allowed to play Holi because of the infection from the . . . the . . .' He struggled to recollect the word. 'The canolavirus. My mother has asked me to keep a distance from everyone and just join my hands and do namaste.'

'Then you must obey your mother,' she replied.

'How old are you, Matangi-Ma?' he asked. 'You see, I dreamt of you last night, and you were celebrating your hundredth birthday.'

Matangi lurched forward to find him and hugged him close. 'I will live forever, my darling, just to be with you.'

Rahul extricated himself from her arms. 'But my friend explained to me that everybody who is born has to die. Like a battery. Robots die too. And trees and plants and flowers and leaves. And the chicken and fish we eat.'

'I get the drift,' Matangi replied. 'But I'm not going to die for a long time. A very, very long time. I will live to be a hundred, I promise I will.' She turned to Lali. 'Get him the gujiyas that Shanta brought. And perhaps there is one last chocolate left in my cupboard.'

Rahul turned to the child. 'Hello! Who's this?' he asked. 'What's your name? I'm Rahul.'

'Riyaz,' the boy replied.

'Pappoo,' said Lali.

'Is he your son, Lali?'

'No, Rahul baba, he is my nephew Pappoo.'

She had brought out a bar of Cadbury chocolate. Rahul broke off a slab and offered it to the boy. 'Happy Holi, Riyaz or Pappoo!' he said. 'Glad to meet you!' He stuffed his mouth with chocolate before turning to his grandmother. 'Tell us a story, Matangi-Ma! The same story you began last time, when my mother disturbed us.'

Matangi sat up straight and smoothed out her hair. 'Many, many centuries ago, when the world was young, there were four young gods, who were brothers. They were immortals; they knew they would never die.'

'I thought everybody has to die?'

'They were immortals; they knew they would never die, that they would continue to live forever in their golden palace in the Himalayas. One day, they heard the sound of a flute and of human voices singing.'

'Do you know what a flute is?' Rahul asked Pappoo. 'It's a bamboo pipe, like what Lord Krishna carries.' He mimed playing a flute, as Lali had shown him yesterday and pointed to the gold-framed print that hung on the wall. Pappoo watched and listened intently.

Lali's phone rang. It was Ritika asking that Rahul be sent down. It was time for him to have his Bournvita.

Rahul hurried out. He had not told his mother that he was going to visit his grandmother.

The glass of Bournvita was sitting on the dining table. He hated milk, it made him feel sick, but his mother just didn't seem to understand. She would pinch him on his arm during the ad breaks, when happy young boys rushed to drink their milk. Sometimes they grew tall and strong before his eyes, right there on the screen, even as she raised her eyebrows and gave him reproving looks.

He tiptoed around the quiet flat. His parents were fighting with each other, he knew they were, even though they hadn't raised their voices. His mother was twirling a strand of hair around with her fingers, as she did when she was very, very angry.

Rahul retreated stealthily. He took the milk from the dining table and threw it down the kitchen sink, saving up the last bit to smear around his lips. Then he returned to their bedroom.

'I've drunk up all the milk,' he said. 'Now can we watch television, please?'

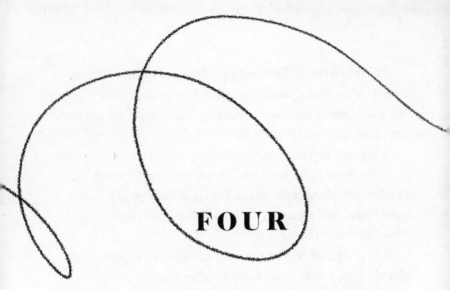

FOUR

Cut to the curfew. The play curfew, the 'Janta Curfew' that the prime minister had imposed.

Nobody was to step out all day, from 7 a.m. to 9 p.m. At 5 p.m., the nation was to assemble to clap and beat pots and pans and cheer for the health workers.

Matangi had listened carefully to the PM's address. It was not belligerent, like his earlier speeches. His voice had a gently wheedling tone; it reminded her of someone, something, from her past. The mithai-wallah in the Kaka Nagar sweet shop who would urge her to buy gulab jamuns?

What did he look like, she wondered, this man everyone seemed to either love or hate in equal measure. She tried to conjure up a picture, from his voice, from his words, from the hiss between his consonants, but she could come up with nothing.

'What does Modiji look like?' she asked Lali. 'Describe him to me!'

Lali giggled. 'He looks like an old man, a buddha baba, with his spectacles and white hair and white beard,' she replied, 'but his skin is as smooth and fair as Kareena Kapoor's.'

'I haven't seen Kareena Kapoor's face, you silly woman,' Matangi said sharply. 'Go and call Suryaveer. He will explain all this to me.'

But Suryaveer wasn't home. He had gone out with Samir, Lali reported, to stock up for the curfew. Everyone was stocking up for the curfew.

'Have we stocked up enough food, Lali?' she enquired, her housewifely instincts suddenly alert.

Lali sighed. 'Mataji, all our food comes from Shanta didi's house. And Munni told me they have enough for a month. Shanta didi told her she does not believe in hoarding. She said it puts prices up in the black market and the poor people never manage to get enough.'

Matangi shook her head. 'We have to look after ourselves first, before we can look after others. We have to prepare for the whole family. Go to the grocery store now and get whatever you can. Rice, atta, oil, butter. And yes, twenty packets of Maggi noodles. Or as many as you can get.'

'I have no money, Mataji, and the grocer will not extend me credit.'

Matangi fumbled under the mattress for the key to her second steel cupboard, the one she always kept locked.

'Open my cupboard,' she said. 'You will find five thousand rupees in a silk pouch. I had put it away after demonetization, after all the fuss about thousand-rupee notes. Take it out and get going. Don't you dare spend any of it on nail polish or Pan Parag or recharging your phone. I will call the shop later to confirm what you spent.'

Lali did as she was told. Matangi's voice followed her. 'I may be blind, but remember I can see everything. I have eyes in the back of my head. I am like a CCTV camera.'

Lali didn't giggle, as she might have done. The old woman scared her sometimes. She wouldn't dare to cheat her, ever.

Suryaveer and Samir had stocked up too. It was an erratically run household, where their oppositional lifestyles collided and made peace with each other. They went together to the supermarket, where Samir raided the shelves for eggs and cereal, and cans and cans of sardines, tuna and baked beans. Suryaveer bought several packets of mung dal and brown rice, tea and coffee, sugar and milk powder, and they were done and ready to wait things out.

Surya came up to meet his mother. He had neglected her since his return from Simla.

'There are hard times ahead, Matangi-Ma,' he told her. 'The poor will suffer, as they ever have. The rich will suffer too, as they never before have. The old will have to look after themselves. Not you, of course! Your children and grandchildren, we are all there for you.'

'Read me a poem, Surya,' she said. 'Nirala or Dinkar.'

The request surprised him. She hadn't asked him to recite a poem for years now, although a shared love for poetry had been an essential part of the bond that held them together.

She couldn't see, but she could sense his smile. She could never forget the happy, lopsided, self-deprecating curve of his lips. She didn't need her eyes, for it sat in her heart, like an amulet or a talisman.

'I shall read you an English poem, today,' he said tenderly. 'Let me look it up on my phone.'

He cleared his throat. '"Song of Myself" by Walt Whitman.' She listened intently.

I celebrate myself, and sing myself,
And what I assume you shall assume,
For every atom belonging to me as good belongs to you.

He looked intently at his mother and was silent for a moment.

I loafe and invite my soul,
I lean and loafe at my ease observing a spear of summer
grass.

The Blind Matriarch

My tongue, every atom of my blood, form'd from this soil,
this air,
Born here of parents born here from parents the same, and
their parents the same,
I, now thirty-seven years old in perfect health begin,
Hoping to cease not till death.'

'You understand that, don't you, Matangi-Ma? Every atom belonging to me belongs to you, for it is you who has made me, physically, mentally, intellectually, emotionally.'

She nodded; of course, she understood.

'I will skip some of it,' he said. 'It's a rather long poem.'

The past and present wilt—I have fill'd them, emptied them,
And proceed to fill my next fold of the future.

He wiped a tear from his eye.

Listener up there! what have you to confide to me?
Look in my face while I snuff the sidle of evening,
(Talk honestly, no one else hears you, and I stay only a
minute longer.)

Do I contradict myself?
Very well then I contradict myself,
(I am large, I contain multitudes.)

Suryaveer was silent for a while after he finished reading. She could imagine his remembered face, reflective in its contours.

'Thank you, Matangi-Ma,' he said. 'I needed to read that poem, to myself, for myself.'

She thought about it for a long time after he left, and nodded at the sense of it.

I contain multitudes.

Outside, on the mango tree, a barbet hammered out its insistent call. Bosonto Bouri, that's what they called the bird in Bengal. The harbinger of spring.

Downstairs, Shanta was dozing off on her sofa when the doorbell rang. She peered through the eye-spy, and there was Mrs Anna Sen, her broad face convex through the glass aperture.

Shanta opened the door, and Anna tumbled in. She was smelling of sweat, and her hair had not been brushed for some time. She looked completely distraught.

'We found our way home!' she said. 'And then I lost him again.'

'I am so glad that you are safe, Anna!' Shanta exclaimed. She was relieved to see her eccentric neighbour, but sensed that this was not the time to ask questions.

Munni brought a glass of water, then a pot of fragrant Darjeeling tea. Shanta poured a cup for Anna, putting in a heaped teaspoon of sugar, then checked herself. 'I hope you are not diabetic, Mrs Sen?' she asked cautiously.

'Not me! I am not diabetic, my dear, but my husband Mr Sen is. Still he eats sweets and more sweets. He hides them in different corners of the house, along with the money.'

Shanta let her go on talking. It would all begin to make sense, she told herself.

'I gather you had gone somewhere together? You and Mr Sen? I hope everything is all right?'

Outside, she could hear the clanging of bells, the beating of pots and pans, the sound of a conch shell. It was five. India was announcing its resilience, its battle with the coronavirus.

Anna sipped her tea slowly. She reached out for a biscuit, which she devoured ravenously, then another.

Shanta had found the slip of paper with Babli Mohan's number. She gave her a missed call, then sent a message. 'Mrs Anna Sen of C102 is with me. Shanta Sharma, C100.'

'So, where is Mr Sen?' she asked Anna conversationally. 'Are you both back home now?'

'Our home is locked up,' Anna replied. 'Those evil servants, they have the keys. All the keys.'

She seemed to have got a grip on herself. She began speaking more coherently now, and the whole heart-breaking story emerged.

They had gone for a walk together in the park outside their house. She was walking at her usual brisk pace, her husband lagging behind, as he always did. When she turned back to check on him, he was sitting on a bench, doubled over with pain and clutching at his heart.

Anna took charge of the situation. She helped him up and they staggered back together in the direction of their house. Seeing their plight, an autorickshaw-wallah sidled up and offered to take them to a hospital.

'I believed him,' Anna said. She was weeping now, wringing her hands as she told the story. 'I blessed him for being such a kind, good man.'

Then the nightmare began. The auto-wallah told them, in broken English, that he would take them to a private clinic run by a German doctor nearby.

Before they knew it, they were deep in the by-lanes of a slum colony. They stopped outside a warehouse of some kind. Everything seemed deserted around.

Another man appeared. They carried Mr Sen inside and pulled her in. Then they went out again and bolted the door from the outside. Anna could hear them laughing and chatting on the phone.

Anna still had her phone with her. Mr Sen never carried one. She tried to call the police, but there was no signal.

The two men came back, carrying some food. She was afraid to eat it, she was sure that it was poisoned, but Mr Sen said that he was hungry and ate it anyway. Oily chhole bhature. She tried to stop him, but when did he ever listen to her?

They took her phone away and began playing cards. They were drinking as well, not much, just some swigs from a quarter bottle of hooch. She thought they were waiting for somebody. Nobody else joined them, not that day.

It wasn't that unbearable, she said. There was a bathroom in the corner, not too dirty. Some Lifebouy soap. A bucket and a towel. There was a mattress to sleep on and a collapsed sofa.

The autorickshaw-wallah took away the small wallet that contained her house keys and five hundred rupees. They had no idea why they had been kidnapped, why they were locked in.

Then a suitcase arrived, with some mismatched clothes. How had they got them? Who had packed them? Mr Sen's shirts and trousers, and underwear. Her skirts, a blouse. No underwear for her! Who sent it?

Anna was in a fury now, banging her hands on the table. Munni brought another pot of tea.

On the third day, another man turned up. He was big and burly and had a handlebar moustache. He told her husband to sign on some stamped paper. It gave him the power of attorney to sell their house. To sell C102. Mr Sen signed it, and told her it was best if she did so as well.

'That man with the moustache—he said he was an honest man, that he was doing it for our good. We were getting too old to live on our own. The servants might decide to murder us. We could use the money he would give us after the sale to move to an old-age home. They kept us there for another week after Mr Sen signed the papers. I was keeping count of the days. They were very nice to us after they had got what they wanted. Chicken curry, rice, even some kebabs. They got us some board games—Ludo,

Snakes and Ladders. The nicer they became, the more I lived in terror that they would kill us. That's how it always is, isn't it? Hansel and Gretel! That what's we felt like— Hansel and Gretel! But they chatted and laughed as though the whole situation were normal. They told us about their children. One had a son in America. Another had a daughter in college. "If you had children, you wouldn't have had to sell your house," they told us, as though everything were normal and above-board.'

She blushed.

'But the worst thing, the *worst* thing, was that I had no extra underwear. So I would wash my panties and then be without underwear until they dried, so worried that somebody would . . . you know, see it. Then they let us free. We panicked! They dropped us near the park, in an Uber taxi. They said we could go home, but if we told anyone they would kill us. So we got home. But no key! No key! No servants, no staff, no Ramu, no Mohan. I have a spare key, I have hidden it safely! But when I looked for the key, I lost him. Mr Sen disappeared. He just disappeared! So I came to you. What should I do now?'

The clanging of the pots and pans, the conch shells, the ringing bells, all were silent. Shanta considered the situation.

'You stay here,' she said to Anna. 'Right here, on this sofa, in this room. With Munni holding your hand. Do you understand?'

Munni nodded her head. Anna took an embroidered cushion and buried her head in it.

20 March 2020. The spring equinox had settled on the calendar a day early. The evenings had stretched themselves out. Shanta set off for the park, ignoring the curfew, to look for Mr Sen.

The park was scattered with yellowed neem leaves. They crunched underfoot as she walked around the deserted jogging path. The green pods of neem, the young niboris, had also fallen to the ground with the unseasonal rain of the previous days. Every now and then she would step on a nibori, and the harsh green smell of bitter sap would rise to her nostrils.

And there he was, in the children's corner, sitting desolately on a low swing, looking at nothing.

Shanta went up to him. He didn't seem surprised to see her.

'Let's go home, Mr Sen,' Shanta said. 'Mrs Sen is waiting for you. And there is a curfew in place.'

There was no reply still from Babli Mohan. Anna seemed confused, relieved, angry, at the sight of her husband.

'Let's find your keys now, Anna,' Shanta said. 'Munni will wait with Mr Sen. I will call my brother down as well. He can chat with Mr Sen while Anna and I go and check things out at C102.'

Surya arrived, dressed in his shorts. Samir came down too, tousle-headed, unshaven. 'I'm growing a beard,' he explained. 'It's a good time to grow things.'

It had got dark. The small garden outside the house was covered in a carpet of rotting neem leaves. An enormous black tabby glowered at them from the front porch. 'I'm friends with this stray cat, this black beauty—I call him Munchkin. I haven't fed him for a week!' Anna exclaimed guiltily. Then she was down on her haunches, searching for something in the rockery.

'Not here! Not there!' she murmured. 'You are really a very forgetful lady, Anna Sen!'

She fumbled next with the ornamental wooden letterbox next to the front door, looking inside it, around it, under it.

There, taped neatly on the underside, was the key, wrapped in brown paper swathed in peeling cello tape.

They entered the house. Shanta switched on the lights and did a round of all the rooms. Everything looked neat, tidy, normal.

Anna had clambered atop a wooden dining table chair to get down some dusty books from a high bookshelf. She brought them down one by one and laid them out like prize exhibits on the glass table before the television set.

'Thank God they are still so dusty!' she said, crossing herself fervently as she spoke. 'Please lock the door, Shanta, will you?'

Six imposing large-format volumes of Gibbon's *The History of the Decline and Fall of the Roman Empire* were carefully opened, one by one, to reveal carefully hollowed-out centres. Each of them held a sealed envelope.

Shanta looked on amazedly as Anna unsealed the envelopes, delicately prising the cello tape and staples apart with a safety pin. Each volume contained wads of banknotes of different denominations. Purple two-thousand-rupee notes in volumes one and two, grey five-hundred-rupee notes in volumes three and four and what seemed to be dollars and greenbacks in volume five. Volume six had some scribbled notes, a letter, a photograph and a pen drive.

'Mr Sen doesn't believe in banks,' Anna explained. 'We have a locker but that just has my rings and brooches. You take this,' she said. 'I would feel safer if you kept this money for us. In case they find out.'

Shanta's mouth fell open in surprise. She certainly hadn't bargained for this. 'I can't keep this money, Anna,' she said. 'We will figure out a way. Let's step back and return to my flat now.'

Anna Sen brought out a capacious handbag and put the packets of money in, bundling them in a silk scarf. All except the letters and notes, which she carefully deposited back into volume six. She climbed on to the chair again and Shanta helped her put the books back where they had been.

They returned to C100. Surya and Mr Sen were locked in an intense conversation.

'Mr Agastya Sen has some fascinating stories to share!' her brother exclaimed. 'He should be writing a book. His memoirs would make for a fascinating read.'

Shanta checked her phone. There was a missed call from Babli Mohan. 'We need to report this terrible incident straightaway,' she said with concern. 'You must file an FIR. Anna told me that your abductors made you sign some legal papers regarding your property.'

'Anna told you, did she?' Mr Sen asked, looking almost amused from under his rimless glasses. 'Those thugs—I know how to deal with them. I could see that Anna was afraid, as was only normal under the circumstances, but I was observing the situation carefully. I'm a trained diplomat, remember. I've been in a hostage situation before, when I was posted in Uruguay, and I'm proud to say that I talked my way out of it. But that's another story!

'As for the papers they asked me to sign—I'm left-handed, but I used my right hand and a completely different cursive script, slanting leftwards. Those papers will never stand up to the scrutiny of even the most demented lower courts. As they say in Sanskrit, "*tatha kim?*"'

They listened to him, amazed.

'I will speak to my lawyer tomorrow before I decide what to state in my FIR, if at all I decide to file one. In any case, there's a legal lockdown along with the rest of this mess. I will discuss the implications of the situation with you, if I may, Suryaveer, after I have spoken with my lawyer.'

Suryaveer couldn't stop laughing. 'Let's have a rum, Shanta, to cheer Mr Sen and his devious diplomatic mind!'

'May I have a single malt instead, should that be available?' Agastya Sen asked tentatively. 'It would be good to calm my nerves, after all this.'

A bottle of wine, some Old Monk, a bottle of Glenlivet. The clink of ice. The evening ended well.

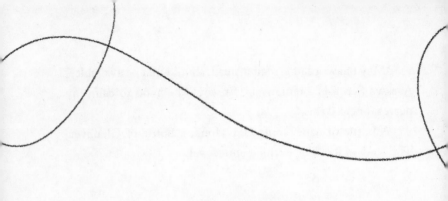

FIVE

The days of the lockdown—there was a sense of timelessness to them. Suryaveer and Samir were sweeping the leaves off their end of the road. The scratch of straw brooms could be heard on the concrete, with no traffic or street sounds to disturb it.

'Surya . . .' said Samir, 'I've been thinking about this place all this week. I can't seem to think of anything else. I need to know about my father. Who he was. How I came to you.'

Surya's face changed. It became cautious, contemplative. 'Your father,' he said. 'Your father was my comrade, my amigo.'

He began walking towards the park with swift, silent strides. Samir followed him. They settled down on a bench. Surya reached out for Samir's hand and held it in his. The sky was a brilliant blue, the air purer than they had ever known it.

'I have been waiting for you to ask me this question, all these long years. I've wondered why you never wanted to know.'

'I guess I went for a creation myth explanation, that a great golden bird dropped an egg in your backyard, and that you sat over it with a blue blanket and hatched me! But seriously, I never felt the need to ask you. You are my father, and my mother too. This is my home. Matangi-Ma is my grandmother. Everything felt complete. I didn't want to know anything more.'

Samir looked around him. The breeze was playing with the petunias in their flowerbeds, the marigolds by the hedge. It was all so unnaturally quiet, like in a dream.

'But these last ten days, being at home with you, it's unnerved me. You've changed, Surya, you look sad; you don't smile as much as you used to. I know so little about you, really—who you are, who you were, why you took me on.'

A lopsided smile spread across Suryaveer's face. There was a faraway look in his eyes.

'I loved your father, and your mother too. He was from Nalanda, from Bihar Sharif. Aditya Sharan Jha. He was the brother I never had. I mean, there was Satish, but Addy and I had more than a blood bond. And your mother—she was the most spirited, most beautiful woman out there anywhere. Samira Susan. She was a Mangalorean Christian, a Catholic. We named you Samir, after her.

'I had left the party by then, but they entrusted you to me, should anything happen to them. You are eighteen now. This was in 2001. They were in Bastar together at the time. You were born in Maharani Hospital, Jagdalpur, on 2 October. On Mahatma Gandhi's birthday. I had become a Gandhian by then. It was the only way, I thought, to address the contradictions in our society.'

Samir was sitting on the bench with his eyes closed, as though he were listening to music. He would nod, occasionally, to indicate that he was taking it all in.

'I wanted them to name you Mohan Das, after Mahatma Gandhi, but Addy insisted you be called Samira, after your mother.'

'I hear you . . .' Samir said softly. 'Aditya Saran Jha and Samira Susan . . .' He tested the names on his tongue, as though he were saying a prayer. 'So, Aditya Saran Jha and Samira Susan, my parents, were communists?'

'We were all communists then,' Surya replied. 'In our hearts and minds. But our circumstances, our experiences, our samskaras, made us follow different paths. They brought you to me when you were a baby, swathed in a blue blanket. They asked me to look after you while they continued with their struggle. Then . . . they died.'

Samir shifted away from Surya to the corner of the bench. 'I don't want to know any more, just now,' he said. 'I need to deal with this, first.'

The crows were quarrelling in the neem tree. A squirrel looked at them curiously, then scurried away. Surya looked around at the empty park, the deserted swings. A thin, straggly cat rubbed itself against him and meowed piteously.

'Look around at the trees in this park,' Surya said to Samir. 'The banyan tree, with its sprawling aerial roots, which return to the earth. The ashoka trees, tall and aloof. The neem trees, shedding their leaves, sprouting new ones. The mango trees. That kadam tree there. They are all connected at the roots. They share their sustenance, their nutrients. They speak to each other under the soil, they sing and they weep, and they rejoice together when the rains come.'

A broad smile broke across Samir's face. 'Always the philosopher, Pop! I'll go up and get some milk for this kitty. She seems to be mighty hungry.'

Then they returned to their brooms and began sweeping up the leaves again.

That afternoon, Suryaveer went upstairs to visit his mother. He wanted to tell her about his conversation with Samir, how they had broken the silence about his biological parents.

Satish was sitting with Matangi-Ma. The brothers greeted each other stiffly. Even though they lived under the same roof, a distance had built up between them.

'How's Rahul?' Suryaveer asked. 'And Ritika?'

'They are all fine,' Satish replied neutrally. He didn't ask about Samir.

Lali brought a tray with a teapot and three cups. The child Pappoo was darting around, and she shooed him off. They could hear him driving an imaginary car in the veranda. 'Vrrroom vrrooom!' he went. 'Vrrroom Vrrooom!'

'No tea for me, please,' Satish said with a strained smile. 'I will make a move, Matangi-Ma, now that your beloved firstborn is here with you.'

Surya raised an eyebrow. What was that about?

Matangi sensed his question. 'Satish has been worried about a lot of things,' she said in a conciliatory voice. 'He was sharing his problems with me before you came, that's all.'

'Who doesn't have problems?' Surya replied shortly. 'I'm sure his sob story was accompanied by a request for a loan. Don't deny it, don't protest, I know my little brother as well, perhaps better, than you know your son!'

Matangi didn't confirm or deny this. Instead, she changed the subject with her usual skill.

'I've got something for you, Surya,' she said. A smile broke across her face as she spoke. 'Come with me to the pantry. I will show you!'

She led him to the large refrigerator, which was often stocked with food from Shanta's frenzied bouts of cooking. She felt around for the handle and opened the door, gesturing to the stacked shelves inside. The unmistakable smell of ripe alphonsos wafted out. There were a dozen, perhaps two dozen, mangoes stacked up inside.

Matangi took the fruits out, one by one, stroking them, holding them against her cheek, before she put them back. 'I was worried about my children,' she said, 'all locked up inside their flats, eating the same things again and again and again. So, I sent Lali off on a mission. The first alphonso mangoes of the season, and some kesari and hamam mangoes as well.'

'We are in quarantine, Matangi-Ma,' Surya said reprovingly. 'You shouldn't let that Lali out at all! Who knows where she will float off if she is allowed to be footloose and fancy-free! We have to watch out for infections. This is a cunning little virus.'

Matangi was holding the fruit in her arms, as though they were a bouquet of flowers. It touched Surya to see his mother so happy, and he changed his tone.

'My Matangi-Ma! The cleverest and most nurturing mother in the world!' he murmured. 'Jai Mataji! Annapurna Devi herself!'

She was still fondling the mangoes, breathing them in. She heaped four of them together. 'Get me a bag, Lali, or a jhola, so Surya can take them back with him. Tell Samir I sent them especially for him—the first mangoes of the season!'

Surya told her of his conversation with Samir. 'I have told him the truth about his parents,' he said. 'It was time that he was told.'

'It was time that he asked,' Matangi replied reflectively. 'We were only holding him in trust for them.'

After Surya left, she succumbed to tiredness. She went to lie down on her bed. The afternoon nap was an important part of her rigid routine; otherwise, the days would collapse into formlessness.

The fragrance of the fruit remained with her as she dozed off. In her dreams, she returned to another summer, redolent with the scent of mangoes. They were in the Kaka Nagar flat. It was still the early part of summer, probably May.

The dry heat was like a moving flame around them. She was sucking at a mango kernel. Her husband and children had been offered the more succulent slices and she had saved the leftovers for herself.

'Let's play a game of badminton together!' her husband had said, quite unexpectedly. 'I remember your mentioning you used to be good at the game?'

She couldn't read what was in his mind, and she decided not to delve too deep into it, to take it at face value. In her dream, she had tightened the pallav of her cotton sari around her waist. She didn't possess any sports shoes, so she had kicked off her low-heeled sandals to enter the fray barefoot.

In her dream, her lips were still smeared with the remnants of the mango, an unlikely orange lipstick. There were parrots in the trees, watching them, applauding them. She had won the toss and balanced the shuttlecock on her racquet with insouciant ease. Then she got into the stride of it, her limbs easing out, as the remembered rhythm of the game entered her body.

She was so absorbed in the exhilaration of play, the joy of victory, that she didn't notice, or register, his change of mood.

'You are cheating!' he had exclaimed petulantly. 'Maybe you don't even know the rules of the game!'

She had licked the last traces of mango off her lips. Her shoulders drooped. Her expression became penitent, pleading. 'I'm sorry,' she said cautiously. 'I haven't played for so long. I've just forgotten the game!'

Her husband Prabodh had dropped his racquet, flung it into the dry sparse grass, and walked off the field. There would be consequences.

Lali had brought her tea. Matangi didn't want to drink it. She wanted to return to that memory, that dream, and to resume that match. She wanted a different outcome this time, she wanted to win the set, to defeat him, to show that she could defeat him.

She tried to forget about her husband, about his visitation, his intrusion into the afternoon. She wanted to return to the present, but she couldn't. The smell of mangoes, the smell of summer, had dragged her back.

Her knees were hurting. The aches and pains travelled unpredictably across her muscles, her skeletal system, converging and re-converging at her knees.

She pushed the tea away. 'I don't want chai today, Lali,' she said. 'Just chop up a mango for me, and the child can suck at the kernel.'

Downstairs, Ritika was sitting at the dining table, a corner of which she had commandeered as her workspace. Rahul did his online classes in his bedroom, which somehow had the best reception in the house. Her husband worked from the study, on his large-screen Mac.

Ritika's life was falling apart. The lockdown had made all the fault lines rise to the surface. And now the company she worked for, Compass International, was just a few steps away from going into liquidation.

She was on an official conference call when the doorbell rang. Rahul and Satish were in their rooms, with the doors shut. 'Excuse me,' she told the others in the meeting, as she dashed to open the door. There was Lali, wearing a surgical mask looped at an odd angle, a basket of mangoes in her arms.

'I'm on the phone, Lali! On a call!' Ritika said impatiently. Lali sidled in anyway and placed the basket of mangoes on the dining table, within view of the camera frame.

'Mataji has sent these for you, Satish sir and Rahul baba,' she said, sliding her mask down to speak. She was about to launch into a longer conversation when Ritika shooed her out, locking the door after her.

The meeting was to discuss strategies and options to counter the consequences of the Covid crisis. The bottom had fallen off the travel industry. Richard Branson was asking for emergency financial aid. South African Airways had collapsed. Airplanes were grounded, cruise ships quarantined. Hotels had been commandeered as hospitals. Creditors were not paying up. What was anybody to do?

The faces on the screen were blurred but all clearly very, very anxious. Her boss, the founder and CEO of the company, was the only one who appeared calm.

'Friends and colleagues,' he said gravely, 'friends and colleagues, you will all have to be sympathetic to the situation; you will all have to cooperate with the management at Compass International. Otherwise, we are a sinking ship. We had already incurred catastrophic losses with the Jet Airways lockdown, which has made our situation even more precarious. I count on all of you to be ready to make sacrifices.'

Ritika's heart went out to Girish. They had been together in school, and when he had seen her name and photograph on the job application, he had called her personally and reached out. The package that Compass had offered was substantially higher than she had expected, and she suspected that their school friendship had something to do with it.

'Every challenge is also an opportunity,' Girish Syal continued, mustering a smile. 'I leave you with this thought: every crisis is also a call to innovation. Let's sleep on our conversation today, and each of us can come up with an inventive solution, an out-of-the-box strategy, to steer us out of these troubled waters.' He smiled wanly at them all. 'Ritika, Renu, Arnab, Govind, Asif. I salute you all for your loyalty and commitment. Let's grow wings, let's all learn to fly together!'

Ritika paced restlessly around the room after the call was through. Despite Girish's optimism, there had been a doomsday mood to the meeting. It would signify the end of many dreams, including hers.

Satish emerged from the study, looking distracted.

'Should I make you some tea, sweetheart?' he asked. 'You look troubled.'

He looked at her concernedly. There were dark circles under her eyes. The white roots of her auburn-tinted hair had begun to show prominently, giving her a raccoon-like look. She was wearing her night-suit pyjamas with a smart white shirt, with a slash of dark lipstick across her taut face.

Ritika hugged her husband and held him close. 'I don't know what to do!' she exclaimed. 'Everything is collapsing around us. How long can we hide here in this flat while our world comes apart?'

He sat her down on the sofa beside him. 'No, honey, no! The world will come together again, and our world too. Let's count our blessings, shall we?'

'Let's take stock first, of all that's going wrong,' Ritika replied. 'I shall probably, almost certainly, lose my job. The travel business will go kaput. Become history. Nobody else will hire me.'

'I'm here to look after you,' Satish said. His voice had a hint of panic in it. 'People always need accountants, and lawyers, and doctors, and dentists . . .'

She hugged him again. 'New software will eat away at accounting jobs. Artificial intelligence will take over everything. Doctors and dentists need living patients!' She managed a smile. 'I'm getting carried away. I know you will be all right, you will. We are lucky to have you as the breadwinner in our family. It's not a joke to be senior partner in such a well-regarded firm!'

It was Satish's turn to look worried. 'Things are not always what they seem, Ritika,' he said softly. 'There is that foolish investment I made, and Mr Gupta is being very difficult. He is surely up to something, I know he is, and he will use this crisis to create more problems, to escalate some pending issues.'

Rahul peeped in from his room, sensed the tension, and retreated inside again.

A fierce tone entered Ritika's voice. 'And then there's my son. Our son. Matangi-Ma's only grandchild. The only real Sharma in the bloodline to take the legacy forward. But Surya—Surya will leave everything to that Samir. And Shanta—your sister Shanta will probably leave everything to her cats!'

Satish looked at her warily. He knew his wife when she got into one of these moods.

'And there's your mother. She has all those FDs in the bank. We all know how much she has! But will she ever part with any of it? Even a bit of it?'

'Calm down, Ritika,' he said helplessly. 'You know she gave us that loan—which we never returned.'

'Well, she is your mother, not a banker, or a moneylender,' she countered.

'You know, sometimes I think she will outlive us all,' Ritika continued recklessly.

Satish stared at her. His hand rose in the air, palm open, as though to slap her. He looked at his hand, with surprise, with concern, then slowly let it drop to his side. He looked at her pleadingly.

'I hope she never dies,' he said. 'I hope Matangi-Ma lives to be a hundred, or a hundred and twenty, or whatever age the gods grant her.'

Ritika turned away and made for the kitchen, where she made a conspicuous clatter with the utensils. She knew she had crossed a line. She knew Satish would forgive her. It was this virus. It was these damned times.

Rahul was playing Mario. He thought he had outgrown the videogame, but it was comforting to re-encounter the familiar figures, those fears and challenges, of his younger self.

Mario stood in his perpetual blue overalls and red shirt. Rahul listened to the well-remembered tune with delight, as he navigated the joys and terrors of the mushroom kingdom.

There was a new Super Mario Maker 2 edition out. He would ask his mother to get him one. Or his Papa.

Were there any Coronavirus games available, he wondered. He would research them on the net. It would power up the skills he needed to cope with future pandemics.

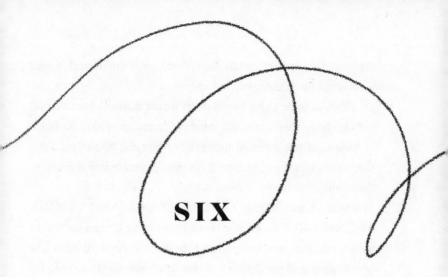

SIX

Matangi could smell the flavourful mangoes. The taste had exploded inside her, into its component flavours and the memories they carried. Ever since she had started losing her sight, each object, every sensory experience had acquired an echo remembrance. It was as though her mind was trying to relocate its visual cues into new clusters of association.

Mangoes made her think of parrots. She thought, now, that she could feel the flapping of wings. Perhaps a beady-eyed parrot, feathered in green, was examining her intently?

'Lali, Lali!' she called, but Lali didn't answer. 'Lali!' she tried again.

The child materialized. Pappoo. Riyaz. 'Do you want something, Mataji?' he asked.

'Is there a parrot flying around my head? Flapping its wings?' She could sense him, looking intently around her.

'No, Mataji, no parrot. Nothing. Not even a fly, or a mosquito.'

'You are a good boy,' she said gently. 'Now go back to do whatever you were doing.'

Matangi re-entered the imagined spaces within her. She listened to the beating of her heart, to its irregular rhythm. She visualized the rivers of blood that coursed through her tired body. She breathed deeply, in and out, in and out, through one nostril, then the other, as Baba Ramdev had instructed on television.

This is where she lived, deep inside herself. Her family, her children, their children, inhabited another sphere, of light, of vision, of the external interplay of images. She could 'see' too; of course, she could, perhaps deeper and better than all of them, but differently.

The cuckoo clock. CUCKOO. CUCKOO. CUCKOO. CUCKOO. CUCKOO. She clicked her tongue against the roof of her mouth, to centre herself, to return to the present. She thought of mangoes and parrots and all the meals she used to cook, for all those years. All the flour she had kneaded, all the chapatis she had rolled out. She thought about it. Fifty years multiplied by 365 days multiplied by twenty chapatis a day. She struggled with the numbers, summoning up the rusty multiplication tables she had 'by-hearted' at school. That was 3,65,000 chapatis. It amounted to something, counted for something.

She was seized by a sudden sense of purpose, a lightness of being. Her knees were still hurting, but she invoked her secret reservoir of strength to get up, to sit up. The aluminium walker was parked near her bed, and she clattered her way to the kitchen.

Lali returned to find Matangi leaning into the open refrigerator, inhaling the scent of the mangoes. She began giggling uncontrollably at the sight.

'Mataji! How did you get here?' she asked, between further spasms of laughter. 'I suppose you will tell me that you have come here to cook us dinner?'

Matangi continued feeling the fruit, fondling it, then stacking the mangoes back in some obscure order. She didn't turn to look at Lali, but her voice was cool, firm and pleasant when she replied. 'That is exactly what I'm going to do, Lali. Not dinner, but I'm going to make some laddoos for my family. It's the least I can do for them during this lockdown.'

Lali's mouth fell open in astonishment. What kind of mad joke was this?

'Do as you are told, Miss Lali,' Matangi continued, a note of amusement in her voice. 'Take out the ghee, the besan and the sugar from the rations I sent you to buy. And yes, some cardamoms from my cupboard.'

Lali look alarmed.

'Do as I say,' Matangi insisted. 'I will teach you how to make laddoos. You can make them for your husband when you get married, and your children and grandchildren after that.'

Lali brought out the ingredients from the cache of food Matangi had put aside for the lockdown. She measured out the ghee, the gram flour and the sugar, as instructed. Two large spoonsful of ghee in the pan, then the besan.

Matangi stepped forward. 'I will stir it myself,' she said. 'The secret of a delicious laddoo lies in how skilfully it is roasted and stirred. You can watch me do it.'

She steered herself in front of the burner. Lali was completely unnerved by now. Mataji was blind, they all knew that she was blind, but it was almost as though she had some mysterious secret vision. She began stirring the batter slowly, deliberately, completely intent on her task.

The fragrance of the roasting gram flour filled the kitchen and floated out to the veranda.

Just then, suddenly, a low rumble rose as though from the bowels of the earth. The kitchen stool started chattering to itself. A steel glass tumbled off the shelf. A teacup rolled away to land on the floor. The pan of roasting ghee and besan tilted over, striking Matangi on her wrist. She winced, then suppressed a scream. Lali took hold of her and of the pan. She switched the burner off.

The kitchen stool had stopped rattling. The pan sat still on the burner. The teacup had ceased its adventure and settled in a corner.

Lali was in a panic. She led Matangi back to her room. 'Let me phone Shanta didi and get you some Burnol!' she exclaimed.

'There is no need, Lali,' Matangi responded firmly. 'Why must Shanta know everything that goes on here? Get me some toothpaste from the washbasin. That will heal the burn.'

Lali did as she was told. Matangi smeared the toothpaste over her wrist and arm, over the angry red welts that were rising there.

'Now go back to the kitchen,' Matangi said, 'and get on with the laddoos. Roast the besan gently, then sieve in the rest of the sugar. They will have become lumpy with this interruption, but what to do! Knead in some more ghee. Then spread it out in a steel thali and let it cool.'

Lali set off for the kitchen. Matangi sat quietly on her bed, trying to control her tears.

She could remember that other earthquake. She was back in Dibrugarh, with her parents. The dangling lightbulb. The wooden rafters. The darkness. Her father. DCP Matang Singh Kashyap. The late Matang Singh Kashyap.

She wept, then composed herself again. It was all so long ago. This was now.

Shanta had rushed up to check on her mother. 'The earthquake,' she whispered. 'The earthquake! Are you all right? Where's Lali?'

Matangi had covered the burns on her wrist and arms with her sari pallav 'I'm fine,' she said. 'I've been through earthquakes before.'

'It was just 3.5 on the Richter scale,' Shanta continued, 'but the epicentre was right here, in east Delhi. The earth is angry with us, as she has every right to be!'

'We hardly felt it here,' Matangi said. 'I didn't even notice it, to be honest.'

'What's that smell?' Shanta asked, sniffing distractedly as she spoke. 'I can smell something cooking.'

The Blind Matriarch

Matangi smiled. 'I'm teaching Lali how to make besan laddoos. You used to love my laddoos when you were children. I will send them down later, for you, for Surya, for Satish, once they are done. Shanta beti, I'm tired today. I want to rest. Why don't you come back later? Or you could send Munni to take the laddoos down.'

Later, after the laddoos were moulded into delicious roundlets and left to cool, Matangi asked Lali to take out her long-sleeved kaftans, the ones she had never worn, from the cupboard. 'The weather is changing,' she explained, 'and it's always best to be careful, what with the mosquitoes returning. Besides, there is no need for the children to get to know that I have burnt my arm; it would just cause them unnecessary anxiety.'

Lali was sent down with the laddoos with instructions to stop at every floor and hand over the packets for Satish, Suryaveer and Shanta. Matangi wandered over to the balcony, looking out at the silent street below with her sightless eyes.

She found herself repeating the well-remembered lines from Dinkar.

Saubhagya na sab din sota hai
Dekho, aage kya hota hai?

What would happen now, she wondered, after this whirlwind of disease and devastation ran its course? Would she be alive to see it, to steer her children and grandchildren to safety? There were no answers anywhere any more.

Shanta was cooking when the policewoman, Babli Mohan, arrived at her door. She was wearing a plastic visor, which she took off when she entered, replacing it with a mask.

'Hello, dear,' she said cheerfully. 'May I impose on you for a cup of tea? I had to visit the Sens next door, and thought I would catch up with you as well.'

Shanta took off her flowered apron and handed the policewoman a bottle of hand sanitizer. 'I'm cooking for my NGO,' she said. 'We supply two hundred meals a day to the shelter homes we support. Someone from the team comes home every day to pick up my contribution. They have a pass, of course.'

Babli Mohan nodded her head approvingly. 'It's good ladies like you who keep our society moving forward,' she said. 'I have come to you because I am very worried on account of Mr and Mrs Sen. Senior citizens . . . I'm not sure how much they can take care of themselves. They sounded confused when I spoke to them.'

Shanta gave a considered reply. 'I send food to them every few days. My assistant Munni, who delivers it, assures me they are doing all right.'

'An interesting thing happened recently,' Babli Mohan continued in a conversational tone. 'You know, of course, from the papers that the crime rate has dropped dramatically.' She beamed proudly, as though she were somehow personally responsible for this. 'The crime rate is down because the city is in lockdown. But there are some nefarious thugs and goons.' She seemed to relish the phrase and repeated it for effect. 'Some nefarious thugs and goons who will use the fear and panic of the pandemic to cheat people, to loot them in broad daylight.'

Shanta wondered what she was leading up to, and why she had decided to stop by.

'There is a gang operating across Delhi,' Babli continued portentously. 'They call themselves the mask and moustache gang. MMG.' She nodded again. 'Yes, MMG. It is headed by an autorickshaw driver and masterminded by a photocopy-wallah who has a stall outside the Karkardooma court and specializes in fake documents. They have come up with a new gig during the pandemic. They enter people's homes wearing biohazard suits and announce that they have been sent to take them into quarantine. When their victims protest that they are asymptomatic and have no history of travel, they insist on fumigating their homes. Only it isn't disinfectant but chloroform that they spray from their nozzles, before decamping with whatever valuables they lay their hands on. They make their getaway in a sealed delivery van for which they have a fake city-pass, for delivery of essential goods.'

Shanta was getting tired of her rambling story. 'I have to get back to the kitchen, Babliji,' she said politely. 'We are in the middle of cooking our quota for the shelter homes.'

Babli Mohan inhaled the smell of vegetables and rice wafting in from the kitchen. 'I haven't had the time to cook since this Covid business began. The maid who used to come and help me isn't allowed inside any more. My brother is a medical intern. He keeps all sorts of hours, like me. My aged mother lives with us. She is strict vegetarian. I cook dal and potatoes for her every three days. My brother and I, we live on fried eggs and omelettes, and bread, whenever we get it.'

'I will pack you some food in a tiffin carrier,' Shanta said. It was an automatic response with her, to cook for people, to feed them.

Babli Mohan's eyes lit up. 'That would be a real treat,' she said. 'But before you go back to the kitchen let me tell you why I came to see you. I've been wasting your time, going on about other things.'

Her demeanour had changed. She was once again the focused professional, speaking about her job. 'When we raided the MMG, we found a phone there. In an empty warehouse, which they grandly call their "headquarters". A battered old phone. Mrs Anna Sen's phone. I took it to her today, but she denied all knowledge of how it got lost, how it landed up there.' She smiled. 'But the police know how to find these things out—a little danda therapy on the goons of the so-called MMG is all that's needed,' she said, a hint of merriment in her eyes. 'We got Mrs Sen to record a statement, but it's full of holes. She contradicted herself at every turn. And that husband of hers, he just kept smiling. Wouldn't say a word. I can't understand how he could have been a responsible government servant—an ambassador, no less! Do tell me the whole story, if they tell you. And watch out for them, they are old and alone. As I know you will!'

Munni had emerged with a tiffin carrier in her hand. Babli Mohan gave them both a smart police salute. 'I hope you will tell me what happened with the Sens,' she said. 'In any case, my colleagues will be in touch with you. Cheerio!'

Shanta's cat, normally housebound, was missing since the morning. She set out to search for Trump, in the street, in the park. Everything outside was eerily quiet. The Residents Welfare Association had locked off one of the entrances, and a lone guard was stationed at the other gate, some distance from C100.

The park had returned to nature. Leaves had piled into peaks and hillocks. Queenie, the stray dog who was the colony mascot, was ensconced on a pile of leaves, surveying her abandoned kingdom.

'Trump!' Shanta called cautiously. 'Trump! Trump! Miss Trump! Where are you, Missy Trump?'

A bat swooped overhead from under the fig tree. An owl hooted. Shanta made another round of the paved walking track, then ventured into the thicket of trees and bushes near the pump room.

There was no breeze, but one of the swings in the children's area was swinging eerily, as though it had been inhabited by a ghost presence.

'Trump!' she called again. 'Missy Trump, Mummy is missing you!'

She glimpsed a movement in the bushes and shone her torch on it. The bushes had been lined with plastic bags to carve out a shelter. A man's face emerged, staring at her. Then a child came out from behind him, and a woman. They stared at Shanta with curiosity and surprise, as though it were a wildlife encounter.

'What are you doing here, brother?' Shanta asked the man.

'We are hiding here for the night, Madamji,' the man replied. 'We will leave at dawn and set off for our village. This city is no place for us any more.'

'Where is your village?'

'Village Bhadauli, District Bahraich,' he replied steadfastly. There was a wealth of pride in his voice.

'And have you eaten?'

He looked down at his feet and said nothing. It was the woman who spoke up.

'We ate some nashta this morning,' she said. 'I am all right, but this child, she is hungry.'

'Stay here, behind the bushes,' Shanta said. 'I don't want the security guard to catch sight of you. I will return with some food. For your journey to Bhadauli.'

Shanta went home and asked Munni to roll out twenty soft chapatis and smear them with ghee. 'Wrap them in foil,' she instructed, 'with some salt and onions.'

They were waiting behind the bushes when she got back. She had carried some masks and sanitizer with her as well, and an envelope with five hundred rupees in hundred-rupee notes.

'May God protect you, sister!' she said, then set off again, searching for the cat.

Was it too late to visit the Sens? Best to put it off until the morning. She had promised ACP Babli Mohan she would watch out for them, just as she had promised Agastya Sen she would keep his secret.

The money Mrs Sen had left with her was kept in the safe in Suryaveer's flat. That too would have to be retuned, once this lockdown was over. It had been extended for another fortnight now, and they would just have to carry on, until then.

She tried to remember that other life, before the lockdown. A blanket of anxiety had descended over her in the last week, like a low fog. How would this pandemic resolve itself without further wounding the soul of India? How?

She thought of the couple hiding in the bushes, of their dignity, their quiet strength.

'May God protect you, sister!' she had said. Where had that come from, she wondered. She had never believed in God. She still didn't.

Yet something was changing within her. She found herself clinging to remnants of faith from her childhood. The pantheon of gods and goddesses that had adorned the walls of the government flat in Kaka Nagar had been visualized through framed prints and calendar art. That was how she thought of them—calm, beautiful, unperturbed. The angry goddesses, the 'Ugra' incarnations, had never found a place on her mother's walls. Her Bengali friend Shutapa's house was adorned with images of the goddess Kali, her bloodstained tongue hanging from her mouth, a garland of skulls strung around her neck.

Matangi would observe all the Hindu festivals—Holi, Diwali, Navratri—and dutifully follow the prescribed rituals, but without much enthusiasm. But the gods were there always, for Shanta, in her team, so to speak. She gave them respect, and a distant affection, along with a detached suspicion that they didn't really exist.

During the nine sacred days of Navratri, a pious neighbour had started broadcasting the Hanuman Chalisa over her music system at seven every evening. The well-remembered verses had reached out to some locked corner of her heart. Something about the twilight, the silence, the resonance of the sonorous recital, provided her with solace. The thought of the monkey god, always strong, always kind, always pragmatic, left her frayed nerves soothed and restored.

Some of the other more secular neighbours had protested, and the daily broadcast was halted. Shanta had found herself humming the Hanuman Chalisa under her breath and discovered to her utter astonishment that she had not forgotten a single one of the forty rhythmic verses that comprised the long prayer. She had chanted it when she was young to keep the demons of childhood away, the ghosts and ghouls and midnight fears, the terrors emanating from her parents' bedroom. It had lingered in her heart, in her breath, and returned to give her calm and courage in these unimaginable times.

Shanta found herself thinking about Babli Mohan, and then began worrying about the Sens next door. She decided to make a quick check on them, as she had promised the policewoman, and keep a look out for Trump as well.

Anna Sen opened the door a crack after she had rung the doorbell twice. Had she been drinking? She was staggering slightly, and her words seemed slurred.

'This is much too late to turn up at our doorstep!' she said. 'We were about to go to sleep. We are old people, you know! Maybe tomorrow is better to talk.'

'Sorry, Anna,' she replied. 'I just wanted to check if you had got your phone back. The policewoman had come to my flat. She told me about the mask and moustache gang and all that!'

Just then, she heard an unmistakable meow. It was a cry for help. It was Trump. Shanta would recognize her melodious meow anywhere. Across the universe.

'Do you have a cat there with you, Anna?' she asked.

Anna Sen's face changed and assumed an unrecognizable expression. 'There is no cat here,' she said, 'I have no pets', and was about to shut the door when Shanta wedged her foot at the doorstep and lunged in, pushing the older woman aside.

And there was Trump, looking impatient and troubled. She was seated on the dining table, which she was never allowed to do at home. Mr Sen was nowhere to be seen.

Shanta took hold of her pet and stroked her tenderly. 'Let's go home, Miss Trump,' she said tenderly. 'Away from this mad cat-napper.'

She left without saying another word to Anna, who watched her departure impassively. Everything about life was getting more and more perplexing, and this was just one more baffling fragment of the overall puzzle.

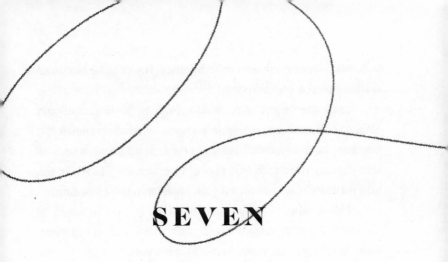

SEVEN

Samir hadn't stopped thinking about his real parents ever since Surya had told him about them. He had grown up with his adoptive father, his grandmother and his aunt Shanta, and never questioned it or thought it different from other people's families. He had never asked why Surya was not married, or who his mother was, though the thought had sometimes crossed his mind.

It was only now, during his first term in college, that the question of his biological parents began to intrigue him. There was a paper on genealogies that involved listing out three generations. He had written his grandmother's name, and that of his father. They were working in groups, or 'sets' as his tutor called them. A particularly pretty girl in his set asked him if he was adopted.

'I suppose so,' he had said.

'I'm so sorry,' she had responded, looking stricken at having asked him the awkward question.

There were some in the group whose parents were divorced, but they were never given the sort of scrutiny that he received during the ancestry project. The days of lockdown left Samir free to fret and brood about his 'real' parents. After his father told him about his biological father, Aditya Sharan Jha, and his mother, Samira Susan, he had resolved to find out more about them and their families. It was to be his secret quest, a search for his roots.

Samir went upstairs to Matangi-Ma to begin his primary research. He sat down beside her and inhaled the particular bouquet of rose-scented talcum powder and jasmine hair oil that he associated with her. He held her wrinkled hands in his, and played with the coral ring she wore on her middle finger.

'Tell me about my real parents, Matangi-Ma,' he asked, in a voice laden with seriousness. 'I want to know all about them, now that Surya has opened up about the past.'

'Your father was only waiting for you to ask him, Samir,' she replied. 'As I was. What can I say? Where should I begin?'

She fondled his face, feeling his young whiskers, the soft tender beard he had sprouted.

'She came to see me, here,' Matangi continued. 'Your mother Samira came to see me, when they left you here, with Surya. My eyesight had already failed by then; I could not see her, but I could sense from her presence that she was an extraordinary woman, brave and beautiful. I asked her to sit here beside me, just as you are sitting now. I held her face in my hands and read it, feature by feature. Her nose was straight and slim, and she wore a tiny nose ring on it. She had soft skin and a voice like an angel.'

Samir listened wonderstruck. She had sat here, where he was sitting. In flesh and blood.

'A voice like an angel,' she continued. 'And I am sure she is blessing you from heaven every day.'

Samir was overcome by emotion. He thought of her, of Samira, she of the slim nose and tiny nose ring, and how she must have sat here with Matangi-Ma and entrusted him to her. His eyes brimmed over and a tear fell on her withered arm. She continued stroking his face.

'What sort of hair did she have?' Samir asked. 'Was it long or short? Straight or curly? Brown or black?'

Matangi stretched out her fingers, as though she were trying to retrieve some memory from them. She considered his question for a while before replying.

'She had thick, curly hair, up to her shoulders. I don't know about the colour. I never saw it, with my eyes.'

That made him weep even more. He fought back the tears and stayed silent. He didn't ask Matangi about his father, about Aditya Sharan Jha. He wasn't ready for that, not yet.

His grandmother stroked his hand again. 'I have something waiting for you, Samir. It's something I have kept for you, all these years that I have been waiting for you to ask me about your mother. About Samira.'

She fumbled for the keys she kept under her mattress. The elaborate silver keychain was shaped like a peacock. She felt the keys and identified the right one.

'Go to my steel cupboard, the one I always keep locked,' she instructed. 'Open it gently with this key. The lock gets stuck sometimes. On the second shelf from the bottom, you will find a bundle of yellow cloth, tied up with a thick yellow string. Bring it here to me.'

Samir did as he was told. The packet was precisely where Matangi-Ma had told him it would be. He marvelled at how organized her cupboard was. The bigger bundles were in the higher shelves, the smaller ones below. A stack of folded shawls, wrapped in individual sheets of plastic, were piled to one side. The steel almirah smelt of cloves and cardamom, and another familiar smell he couldn't quite identify.

Samir returned to where Matangi was seated, still as a statue. He handed her the bundle of yellow cloth. She untied the thick yellow string, deftly untangling the intertwined knots. There was a cardboard box inside.

'This is for you,' she said. 'Your mother left it for you. For when you were ready.'

Samir opened the box with trembling hands. His eyes were blurred with tears.

There was a photograph inside. A colour photograph, fading slightly at the edges, of a beautiful young woman. She had slanted eyes and a tiny nose with a gold nose ring perched on it. There were hills in the background, a blue sky with clouds.

Who had taken the photograph? Her father? Or perhaps his father? Had they gone for a picnic, on a day filled with laughter? What had happened to them, after that day? Why had they abandoned their only child?

There was something else in the box as well, wrapped up in yellow handmade paper. He opened it carefully, tenderly, and found a gold chain, with a gold cross, encrusted with what seemed like diamonds.

His grandmother was observing him with every fibre of her being. He could sense her taking it all in—his quickened breath, his suppressed tears. His wonder.

She smiled. She did not ask him about what was in the box. She patted him on the cheek, then on his head, like a blessing.

Instinctively, he bent down to touch her feet. 'I must go now, Matangi-Ma,' he said. 'Here are your keys. Thank you for keeping this safe for me all these years.'

Samir locked himself in his room and drew the curtains. He propped up the photograph of his mother, of Samira Susan, and lit a candle before it. It was a scented candle, and the comforting smell of vanilla filled the room, calming and soothing him.

'So, here I am, Mummy,' he said softly. 'Your son Samir.' He held the gold chain with the diamond cross in his hand, feeling the weight of it, the cross weave of the thick chain, before he placed it beside the candle, before the photograph. 'Your son,' he repeated. 'I'm sure you will know and understand me better than even I do. I want to tell you, Mummy, that I respect your choices. You left me in safe hands; you left me because you had to tread your path, a path where you couldn't carry me with you. And tell Aditya—my father Aditya—that I will come to him later, when I'm ready. I'm sure you are both hanging around together, like you always did. I just want to be with you, first. Alone with you, as I was when you first carried me around in your tummy.'

Samir imagined his mother holding him, kissing him. He imagined that she was baking him a cake, and that the vanilla smell was wafting in from the oven. He picked up the gold chain from where he had placed it, before her photograph, and wore it. The gold, cold yet warm, felt unfamiliar against his skin.

Then he fell asleep. It was late in the evening when he awoke. Surya was knocking on the door to check on him.

The curtains were still drawn. The vanilla candle had spluttered out, and the scent of vanilla was replaced by the acrid fumes of the dying candle. Surya entered the room, and Samir switched on his bedside lamp. He saw the photograph, propped against the bookshelf, and nodded towards it, as though acknowledging an old friend. He did not say anything.

Samir was on his laptop, struggling with an assignment from his online classes. The dog, Dollar, had sensed Samir's mood, and settled at his feet, with his hind legs under the faded velvet sofa.

The door to their first-floor flat was never locked. A small face peeped in. It was his cousin Rahul. 'May I come in, Samir dada?' he asked anxiously.

'Come right in, Rahul, and settle down here with me and Dollar,' Samir responded. Rahul made a cautious petting gesture towards the dog, then sat on the chair opposite the sofa where Samir lay sprawled.

'I need your help, Samir dada,' he said politely. 'I know how busy you must be, but I thought I would ask anyway. It's about homework. An assignment they have given me in my online classes.'

'Of course,' Samir replied. He was extremely fond of Rahul, though somehow he didn't get to see much of him. 'What's the homework? This project they have assigned you?'

'I have to construct a family tree,' Rahul said, his face expressionless, his eyes fixed on the middle distance, as though he were answering a question within a classroom. Then he smiled. 'We are lucky, aren't we, Samir dada, to have such a large family, all in one building? There's only three of us, on our floor, but then I have you, and Surya chacha, and Dollar, and Shanta buaji, and Munni, and Trump, and of course, best of all, Matangi-Ma, and Lali, and now Pappoo.'

He was counting on his fingers as he spoke, first his right hand, then his left, then back to the right hand again.

He flashed another delighted, toothy smile at Samir. 'You will help me, won't you?' he asked again.

'Of course I will, bro!' Samir replied, giving Rahul a high-five. His mother's face floated before him like a visitation. The mother who had been returned to him. This was meant to be. The universe had sent him a message.

'Just mail me the assignment,' he said, 'and we will settle down together and crack it!'

Rahul walked slowly up the stairs that led to the second floor. He was reluctant to return home, and contemplated going up the next flight of stairs to call on his grandmother, perhaps even persuade her to share a chocolate with him.

But his mother would get to know. She would smell the chocolate on his breath, read the expression on his face. She was always angry these days, or upset. There were stacks of dishes piled up in the normally spotless kitchen. Mummy was a good cook, usually, but now that the day-maid could no longer come home because of the virus, it all seemed to have gotten too much for her.

Quarantine. He played around with the word in his mouth. The letter Q had always fascinated him. It was like a cat with a tail. He tried to think of other words that began with a Q but couldn't think of any. Queer? He knew what that meant. Queen. Quiz. Quilt.

His mother. She had always been strict, but also kind and comforting. She had changed, become like Cruella de Vil, or the Wicked Witch of the West. Rahul and his father would skulk around the house like ghosts and avoid looking each other in the eye. They would pretend that everything was normal. But they knew.

There was a glass of milk with Bournvita waiting for him in the dining table. He drank it up in one long gulp; then went to the bathroom and threw up.

Rahul's request had left Samir excited and enthused. He felt that the fates were conspiring to somehow unite him with his mother, with his other family. Yes, he would help little Rahul with his school assignment. And he would pursue his own private project, his personal investigation, into his newly discovered roots.

A great restlessness rose inside Samir, like a tidal wave. He wanted to step out and scream at the sky. He longed to see an expanse of sea, and the horizon beyond, or to feel alone in a crowd, to inhale the diesel fumes in a traffic jam under a flyover. He had stayed confined indoors for almost a month now, except to sweep the leaves in the park. He felt imprisoned in the flat. He had to break out.

Dollar sensed his mood and settled on his lap, panting and drooling his love. Samir pushed the dog away and began pacing restlessly around the room.

The drums. There was a drum set in his room, an indulgent present from Surya on his twelfth birthday. Or was it his thirteenth? A starter drum set, in those days when he had fancied himself a potential rock star. His drum phase had been short and fruitful, before he had abandoned it for photography. But the set remained, in an alcove in his bedroom, an unlikely installation piled high with towels and odds and ends.

There was a bass drum and a pair of dusty cymbals. The main and side snares. The metal drumsticks. The wooden drumsticks. Samir threw the mess of towels away and got going. He held the dusty metal drumsticks in a matched grip and began on the bit of music he knew best, on '*Billie Jean*' by Michael Jackson.

THAK THAK THAK THAK. THAK THAK THAK THAK. His right hand. One and two and three and four. His left hand. One and two and three and four. The cymbals and snare drums responded to his fumbling beat. Soon, he was absorbed by the sound, lost in it. Nothing else remained but the percussion, the primal heartbeat he had known in the womb.

Surya heard him. He peeped in and quietly shut the door. It was time to let the boy be.

Upstairs, Rahul heard the sound of the drums and smiled. Satish was on a call with his ear pods on. Ritika was lying in bed, nursing a migraine. She heard the drumbeat as it travelled up from the floor below. It entered into her head and invaded her with its cacophony, its pointless aggression. She did not, could not, hear the confusion and pain behind it. She covered her head with her pillow and screamed. The insistent beat of Billie Jean drowned her cry. Then she began sobbing before, at long last, falling asleep.

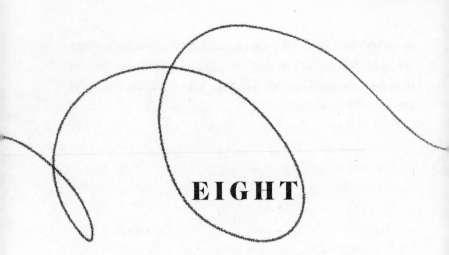

EIGHT

Matangi heard the drums. How could she not? Her keen senses registered them, but for once she was unable to immediately understand the source of the sound. It entered her room from the open window, and she listened intently to the frantic beat. It was too unmusical to be recorded music. Who was hitting the drums so angrily, with so much despair? Why?

The echo resonated in her head long after Samir had ceased and desisted, and entered into the other everyday noises around her. Lali was grinding something in the food mixer in her kitchen; it sounded like a helicopter about to land. The child was playing his vvrroom-vvrrroom games in the balcony. Outside, the birds continuing with their late evening chorus, even though it must have gotten dark outside by now. And in her head, Samir's drums, the clang of the cymbals. Lali had lit a stick of incense in the veranda, as she sometimes did. The fragrance of sandalwood floated in, with the sharp after-smell of commercial agarbatti sticks.

Pappoo rushed into her room in high excitement. 'Mataji! Mataji!' he squealed. 'There's a monkey in the veranda!'

'Tell Lali to hand it a banana,' she said calmly. 'And to lock the kitchen door. Or better still, you do it, young man. Give the monkey god a banana and get the blessings of Hanuman ji, Pappooji.'

He stared at her for a moment, a flicker of doubt running across his young face. 'I am a Muslim, Mataji, and we don't worship monkey gods the way you Hindu people do. The Maulana has explained it all to us. Besides, it's a very big monkey, a langur. I'm just a small child! I'm afraid! I will run and lock the kitchen door, though, as you told me to.'

'Blessings and duas never hurt anybody, Mr Riyaz,' Matangi responded. 'Tell Lali to give the monkey a banana or two if you are afraid.'

That was enough excitement for the day. Matangi covered herself with the thin Jaipuri quilt and curled up, to return to the continuum of her past and the comfort of memory. She drifted into an uneasy dreamscape. She was in an ashram, washing the dishes. The guru, in his saffron robes, had just finished his evening meal. There was a half-eaten laddoo on his plate. She picked it up from the brass thali and ate it. Later, the guru called her into a dark cave, where he was seated on a long, low wooden takht.

'I know you have eaten from my plate,' he said, 'and tasted the fruit of my wisdom. Open your eyes, and you will be able to see what others cannot. Or will not.'

Just then, Lali had switched on the television, very loudly, at full volume. This was, as Matangi knew, one from her bag of tricks to wake her up when she dozed off at the wrong time.

'You haven't even eaten anything, Mataji,' Lali said reprovingly. 'You can't fall asleep on an empty stomach!' She brought her the evening meal, a roti with some vegetables.

The sweet, granular taste of the laddoo was still in her mouth. 'But I've had a laddoo, from the guruji's thali,' Matangi replied, then realized that it had been a dream, that she was awake now.

The news. America. Italy. London. All places she had never been to, would never go to.

The virus. The disease. People dying everywhere. What did the virus look like, she wondered. Lali had tried to explain to her that it looked like a large red or green ball with spikes, but she couldn't picture it. Did the virus have feelings? Was it angry with the world?

The lockdown had not changed her life in any way at all. She couldn't remember when she had last left the flat atop C100. There had been a visit to the hospital some years ago, for a CT scan. Surya had suggested that he and Satish would carry their mother down on a chair. Matangi had rejected the idea in her usual quietly stubborn way and slowly edged her way down, with one hand on the banister and Surya holding the other.

Nothing had changed in Matangi's life, yet the strange and unexpected quarantine had led to all her children being there, in the same house, all the time. She sensed that it was hitting them all in different ways. They were all coping, for now. They were survivors, all of them. It was little Rahul she worried about most. He was the most fragile, the most vulnerable, as a world he had trusted fell apart before him.

Matangi could sense that Lali was getting restless, and Pappoo too. Something would have to be done about the boy, once things returned to normal, if they ever did. He would have to be sent home, or to school if he continued to stay here.

She would ask her daughter, she resolved. Shanta would know what to do. She always did.

In her flat on the ground floor, Shanta too was thinking of her mother. The frantic spells of cooking had come to a standstill, as the various vociferous Resident Welfare Associations had mandated that no cooked food was to be distributed. Her NGO, Women for Peace, was now distributing packets of weekly rations instead.

So, here she was, stuck at home with Munni and Trump, and her siblings perched on the floors above her. She felt strange, grounded, returned into the timelessness of an eternal continuum. She may as well never have left home at all, never made those aborted bids for independence.

The Indian joint family. Theirs wasn't strictly a joint family, in that it had separate kitchens, pockets of privacy. Yet it was worth considering that chicks hatched, birds left their nests, and it was in the nature of things for god's creatures to fly away, to seek new pastures, new horizons.

Shanta had left home when she was eighteen. She had never been good-looking, and her father had been cruel as only he could. 'You are darkish, and plump, and haven't learnt any housework,' he had commented matter-of-factly. 'The only way to marry you off is with a fat dowry. But I'm not ready to do that, no, madam, I'm not.'

Her mother's face. Shanta remembered her mother's face when he said these words.

'My daughter doesn't need any dowry,' her mother had replied. 'Even if she did, I have gold and jewellery and the fixed deposits in the bank from the money my uncle Satish left for me.'

'You and your fixed deposits!' he jeered. 'The money would have doubled if you had let me invest it for you. You are welcome to find a husband for your precious daughter. An IAS officer, I suppose.'

'My daughter will become an IAS officer,' her mother had declared calmly. 'Not the Indian Revenue Service like you, Mr Sharma, but a pucca Indian Administrative Service officer.'

The hatred, the bitterness, that spewed up between them was perhaps the only thing that held them together. Well, she had never gotten married, or made it to the IAS, she reflected, but she had no regrets. Her mother had paid for her college, all of it, from the interest she got on her FDs. She had encouraged her to go to Bombay for the stint at the Tata School of Social Service, and to London, for the degree from SOAS. The fixed deposits were still in the bank, quietly accumulating interest every month, every year.

Shanta had never forgiven her father those words. She had been dry-eyed when he died, looking after the priest's demands, and the ghee and the sandalwood for the funeral pyre, while his broken-hearted sons consoled their mother.

Had Matangi-Ma cried when her husband died? Shanta had no memory of it. She remembered her mother sitting in a corner of the room, on a thin mattress spread out on the floor. The mattress was covered with a crumpled white sheet. Her mother was wearing a white cotton sari. The priest had instructed that she remove her gold bangles, her red lac bangles, her earrings, her bindi, her wristwatch even. She was holding her head in her hands and staring unseeingly at the patterns in the cracked mosaic floor.

The sequence of the past had long since muddled in Shanta's mind. When had she come to know of his other life? The gambling debts. The letters. The office enquiry. His other life, so furtive, so irrelevant, really, all these years later.

It was strange to think they were all here still, at C100, with magnificent Matangi-Ma holding them together, as she had always done.

And things would open up again, the world would return to its old ways, and this oppressive sense of being stuck in a lift which was not moving, which might never move, this would pass too.

The doorbell rang. It was Anna, almost unrecognizable in a fierce-looking black mask, with a bag slung by her side and a cake in her hands.

Shanta let her in warily.

'I made a Polish cake for you, a babka,' she said cheerily, as though their last encounter had been entirely pleasant, as though she hadn't tried to steal Shanta's cat.

'Thank you for the cake, but I don't want it. Please feed it to Mr Sen,' Shanta said firmly. 'And I want to know, I really need to know, why my cat Trump was locked up in your house. That was odd behaviour, inconsiderate behaviour, and'—she couldn't check herself here—'possibly even criminal behaviour!'

Anna Sen was not in the least fazed. 'Mr Sen is diabetic and so he can't have my babka,' she replied. 'As for your cat, your beautiful kind cat—how do you call her, after the American president?—your cat had herself come over to visit me. I shut the door; I didn't let her return, only because her company was making me so happy.'

She took out the bag dangling from her arm and laid out a multi-coloured array of homemade masks on the dining table. There were fashioned from scraps of material Anna must have painstakingly accumulated over the years. There were ten plastic packets, with fifteen masks in each, neatly packed and labelled.

Shanta's heart melted. 'Oh, Anna!' she exclaimed, reaching out to hug her, which of course she couldn't in these times. 'Oh, Anna!'

'These are for the poor, the helpless, the needy,' Anna said loftily. 'You do so much, Shanta, and I wanted to help you in any way I could. And the money—the money we have left for safekeeping with your brother—we will take it back soon after all this is over, and deposit it in the bank. But you are welcome to take 50,000 rupees out of it for your charity. I will count it out and hand it over if you want.'

Shanta was touched. She had misjudged Anna Sen. There was surely some good in every human being, if one dug deep enough. She was also cautious. Anna was clearly unbalanced.

What if her visit was a cunning ploy to abduct Trump, as she had done before?

She picked up the orange ball of cat fur and deposited Trump in her bedroom, locking the door behind her. Anna was munching the laddoos that Matangi had sent for her daughter. Shanta tried to nudge the older woman to leave, but Anna ignored her hints.

There was a soft knock on the door. It was her nephew Rahul, as solemn, as heartbreakingly polite, as ever. He was dressed in his night suit, which had a pattern of blue and pink baby elephants hand-printed on it. His face was covered with a blue surgical mask. He held a large notebook in his hand.

Shanta seized the opportunity. 'I have to help my nephew with his homework, Mrs Sen,' she said firmly. 'You really must get going. And thank you for the masks. We shall distribute them to the needy with your good wishes.'

She sent an overenthusiastic flying kiss in her direction and bundled her neighbour out. Rahul gave her a respectful wave as well, then settled down to devour the remaining laddoos.

'There's a Polish cake, a babka, waiting for you as well, but that's for tomorrow,' Shanta told him. 'Now show me what's in that notebook.'

'It's not homework really,' he explained earnestly. 'Not an online assignment, but a part of the suggested creative curriculum. It's a poem. A poem for our times.'

She wanted to hug him, but the laws of social distancing prevailed. His oversized mask made him look like some small creature from an out-of-date sci-fi film. She couldn't believe that her staid brother Satish and his sour wife Ritika could have produced anyone so delicious.

'So, little man, how are you doing?' she asked. 'Would you like another laddoo?'

'I'm cheating already, Shanta bua,' he confessed. 'I've crossed my sugar allowance. So no more, thank you. I came to see you with a purpose. I've written the first two lines of this poem, and I don't know what to do next. May I discuss it with you please?'

'Of course,' Shanta said, clapping her hands in delight. 'I'm all ears.'

Rahul took off his mask. 'The Lockdown,' he began.

Lockdown, lockup, lock, lock, lock.
Shutdown, shutdown, shut, shut, shut.

Shanta waited expectantly. 'That's all I've written,' Rahul confessed. 'I don't know how to continue and I thought you might be able to help.'

'It sounds wonderful just the way it is!' Shanta said gallantly. 'You could always repeat the lines for effect, like a hip hop poet. And Samir dada could accompany you on the drums. I notice that he has been practising furiously.'

'I'm already working with Samir dada on a project,' Rahul said importantly. 'He is going to help me, and you must too! It's a family tree project.'

Shanta raised her eyebrows. 'We are going to find out more about our family, are we?' she enquired in mock astonishment. 'I will tell you all you need to know, little Rahul, about me, and Munni, and Miss Trump.'

They returned to the puzzle of the poem and read it out loud, together.

Lockdown, lockup, lock, lock, lock.
Shutdown, shutdown, shut, shut, shut.

Shanta thought hard, but nothing came to mind.

'Duck down, duck down, duck, duck, duck?' Rahul suggested.

'That's perfect!' Shanta exclaimed. 'You could leave it at three lines, like an imperfect haiku.'

'What's a haiku?'

'Look it up on the net,' Shanta replied. 'And another poem, perhaps, on the earth? Or families?'

'I'll think about it,' Rahul promised, as he rose to leave. His nightshirt was covered with the remnants of the laddoos, and a single cardamom rested near the button, on the tusk of a blue-pink elephant.

'Shutdown, shutdown, shut, shut, shut,' Shanta whispered to herself as she let Trump out of the bedroom and settled on the sofa to watch the nine o'clock news.

NINE

Matangi had said it just like that, without thinking or reflecting on it. It was as though the words had been put into her mouth, by someone. Something.

'There is a bird,' she had said. 'A green bird. It is hurt. It has fallen off a branch. It doesn't know how to fly. Bring it here, Lali, to me.'

Today, of all days, Lali was not in the mood to indulge her. It was a Sunday, and she hadn't had a day off in months. It was Akshaya Tritiya. It was Ramzan, or Ramadan, as they called it now. Lali was not religious; she was a cynic, almost an atheist really, but in these times it was best to honour all the gods one could.

Matangi was calling to her again. She pretended not to have heard. Age did that to people. They imagined things. They said whatever came into their minds. It was but natural.

Lali was bored of the bland fare that Shanta was sending up in her tiffin meals. She resolved to cook something with some dum in it—with taste and flavour, not the usual lightly sautéed vegetables and dal. She got down to preparing a spicy egg curry. She peeled the onions and minced them painstakingly in a kaddoo-kas. Eight eggs, and some frozen green peas as well.

'Life is like these onion skins,' she told herself. 'Layers and layers of skin, until, in the end, there is nothing. Just the empty tears they leave us with.'

It was not an original thought. She had encountered the lines in a radio play she had once heard, many years ago, but the sense of them had resided with her. They made sense, even more so in these strange times, when everybody was alone with themselves, with their thoughts and memories and regrets and anxieties.

The old lady was calling her again. She pretended not to have heard and put the onions in the mixie to drown out Matangi's gentle, insistent, nagging voice.

Shanta had come up; Lali could hear her, and Munni too. She left the curry to simmer and returned to Matangi's room. She was on the same subject again.

'There is a bird,' she said. 'A green bird. I can see the bird. It is hurt. It is lying under a tree. It doesn't know how to fly.'

Shanta listened patiently. Was the lockdown beginning to get to Matangi-Ma? There was a note to her voice she had never encountered before—childish, petulant, querulous.

'I will go and search for the bird, Mummy,' she said, 'but let's have some tea together first. I will ask Lali to put some of her special masala chai on the boil.'

'Mataji is going on and on about some bird,' Lali sighed. 'I don't know what to do with her. She can be like a little child, sometimes.'

Samir sauntered in. Matangi-Ma stroked his hand, made him sit beside her. 'There is a bird,' she said again. 'An injured bird. It cannot fly. Bring the bird here. It needs to heal.'

Samir was in an upbeat mood. The drumming was going well. He felt he was making real progress. His internet research on genealogies and family trees was going well. The photograph of his mother stood propped against his bookshelf. She smiled at him in his dreams.

The Blind Matriarch

'I will go in search of this mysterious bird, which has sent you such a powerful telepathic distress signal,' he said indulgently. It was always good to step out of the house, whatever the excuse. He put on the cloth mask that Shanta bua had given him, handstitched by Anna.

Samir's gait quickened as he stepped out. He felt a rush of freedom. The confinement was getting to him, even though at another level he had fallen into the lulling rhythm of these strange days.

The street was completely deserted. He began walking around aimlessly. Somebody had been sweeping the leaves, he noted. They lay in neat piles, with the breeze ruffling them ever so slightly.

He passed the Sens' house. The curtains were drawn, except for a patch of light from a corner window.

There was something lying under the streetlight, beside the spreading red cotton tree. A small bird, with its wings spread out, as though it had fallen from a height. It looked frightened and frail, but alive.

Samir's heart stopped. This was more than a coincidence. By some freak accident of the universe, this bird had reached out to his grandmother, sought her mercy. Its plea had been heard.

A large black cat was observing them intently. Samir didn't know the best way to pick up the bird. He called his father, keeping a watch out for the cat as he spoke.

'I'm outside the Sens' house,' he said. 'Come down here. Bring a small towel with you. A hand towel will do.'

The hairs on his arms were standing on end. His palms were sweating. There was something of the moment that had the shadows and textures of other moments, other lives. He didn't know quite how to describe it, but he knew he had been here before, in this moment, in the past, or perhaps in the future, under this streetlight, where he had been sent to pick up this small green bird, shivering and shuddering in the pavement, and to take it home.

Surya arrived, barefoot, in shorts, wearing a black mask. He didn't ask any questions, just picked up the bird tenderly, placed it on a hand towel and breathed gently in its direction. Samir was silent. They were climbing up the stairs when Samir said, in a very quiet voice, that they were to take the bird to Matangi-Ma.

'She knew it was lying there,' he said. 'She told me to find the bird and to bring it up so it could heal. This is so weird. Everything is weird, these days, and this only makes it stranger . . . weirder.'

Matangi had heard their footsteps. She turned her head towards the door, expectantly awaiting their arrival.

Shanta saw Surya enter the room, a bird held aloft in his hands, cradled in a blue hand towel. She felt a sense of shock, and of recognition. Her mother had heard the bird, heard its squeaks for help. That's all there was to it.

Lali said nothing. The old lady scared her, sometimes. It was as though Allah had taken away her eyesight but given her some other faculties instead. Lali's grandmother, the Muslim one, would tell her tales of djinns and ghouls, and creatures who had strayed from the path. They would huddle under a velvet quilt, where she would be overwhelmed by her grandmother's paan-scented breath. She had loved the delicious complicity of those storytelling sessions.

Who knew if it was even a bird? It could be a spirit, or a sorcerer's demonic tool. Or just a winged creature, fallen from its nest. Who knew anything, ever, and more so in this strange time?

Lali went to the kitchen and brought out a medical dropper, which she had washed and kept ready, perhaps for this very moment.

'Shall we give it some water?' she asked. 'That's what my abba used to do, in the village.'

'Just a drop, or it will choke,' Surya said. The bird looked around at them all, at the circle of human faces observing it. It felt the water trickle into its parched beak.

The bird: small, green, with a disproportionately large beak. It was a nestling, not a hatchling; it looked still puzzled by the world. One of its wings was brushed by a wisp of white cotton-silk from the semal tree outside C100.

Samir was looking up 'how to care for an injured baby bird' on Google, but Surya had already taken charge.

'We can feed it a pinch of puréed fruit,' he said, 'tonight or tomorrow morning. That's what birds eat—fruit and worms.'

'I want to hold the bird,' Matangi said. Surya handed it over to his mother. It lay swaddled in blue towelling and peered out incuriously at her. Matangi gently draped her embroidered handkerchief over its tiny body. The bird's bright green feathers stood out against the fraying threads.

'Hello, you little flyaway,' she murmured. 'You called out to me, and now you are here. Do I have to look after you, I wonder, or are you destined to look after me? Our karma is intertwined, you and me, together and alone.'

'The little flyaway is a barbet,' Surya said. 'Only barbets have these distinctive beaks.'

Lali had magically produced a cage. It had been lying in the small storeroom next to the garage, waiting precisely for this day to arrive. It was made of brass, and had a feeding bowl, a bar and a hoop.

'Where did that come from?' Shanta wondered. Then she remembered. A college friend had parked her parakeet with her for a month while she was travelling and never collected the spare cage she had left behind. That was twelve years ago, she calculated, and marvelled at how objects and memories languished and multiplied under the canopy of a joint family.

Lali and Munni cleaned up the cage. The blue hand towel was laid out at the base, and the barbet settled comfortably on it.

Later, in his room, Samir pondered over the sequence of events, of how he found the bird lying on the pavement under the red cotton tree. He remembered the black cat waiting in the shadows, and Matangi-Ma's instructions to search for the bird. He thought of the mother barbet, sitting beside her empty nest, worrying about her chick. Had she seen him carry the bird away in the blue towel? Did she know her child was safe?

He thought of his own mother, Samira Susan, and he wept hot, urgent tears, as though for a new wound, as well as an old ache come suddenly alive.

The tears gave him relief. He brought out a can of beer from the fast-depleting case in the refrigerator and settled down before his laptop for a long stretch of research. He had been compulsively searching for Samira Susan. Several references showed up but none of them could have had any connection with his mother. There was Mrs Samira Susan McBride Burns (1855–1935). He found a singer called Susan Samira, complete with discography. There were others, but nothing that he could associate with the smiling face in the photograph.

He went back to the drums and played a hit-and-miss version of 'Gulabi Ankhen', but was so distracted and disturbed that his own playing began to give him a pounding headache.

Upstairs, Ritika groaned when she heard the frantic beat of drums from the floor below. In the next room, her son Rahul smiled appreciatively. Anything Samir dada did always received his fervent appreciation.

Ritika heaved a sigh of relief when Samir gave up on the drums. She would really have to speak to Suryaveer about it. But all the siblings of this odd family were so prickly, each in their own peculiar ways. She would bring up the subject tactfully, when she could.

She was, Ritika reflected, the only person in the building not related by blood. Lali and Munni were servants, even though they had both been working here long enough to almost qualify as family—almost but not enough. And Samir—the boy remained a mystery to her. She had long harboured the suspicion that Samir had not been adopted at all, but was actually Surya's biological son, from some mysterious secret relationship.

She had never been able to understand the subtle dynamics between the three siblings. Ritika was a single child, and did not have the extended cohort of cousins and uncles and aunts that most of her friends and acquaintances did. There was a relative in Canada, and one in Coimbatore. She was not in touch with either.

Her father had been a senior engineer with Bharat Heavy Electricals Ltd. They lived on the campus of the massive public sector undertaking. It was a sedate, secure life. Her father died the year after Ritika got married. Her mother lived alone for some years. She became forgetful and was diagnosed with dementia, then with Alzheimer's.

It had been a nightmare. Another city, another state, with no security blanket of brothers and sisters, aunts and uncles, to help her out. Satish had been magnificent. He had helped find a nurse, a Konkani lady from Bangalore, through a client. Sister Bokade had looked after her mother devotedly.

Ritika visited her once a year, with Rahul. She didn't stay with her mother during these visits, in her small flat in the outskirts of Bangalore. They checked into a spotlessly clean hotel nearby. Rahul would observe his grandmother with wide-eyed wonder. His nani was completely different from his dadi, his Matangi-Ma. She would laugh without reason sometimes, or remain silent for the longest time. She had a kind, unwrinkled face and the sweetest smile he had ever seen. She would make him lie down next to her on the soft mattress, covered with floral bedsheets. She seemed in so many ways like a child herself.

Ritika had not visited her for six months now. Sister Bokade had died last summer, and there was no option but to register her mother in a nursing home for Alzheimer's patients. It was not cheap, but it was run professionally, and with integrity, by a retired army doctor.

How would she pay for the nursing home now? She did not want to ask Satish for money. Her savings would keep her going for a while, but for how long?

The drums and the beer had given Samir a headache. He returned to the computer, determined to stay with his search. He was typing out her name on Facebook now. Samira Susan yielded a surprising number of leads. But it was bound to be a futile quest, he told himself. His mother would still be young if she were alive today, but she had belonged to another time, another age. The internet had just begun to weave its web when she died. He would have to look for another way to track her.

Perhaps it would be better just to let things be. To put the photo in a silver frame and place a flower before it every day to honour her memory. A white rose, a white mogra.

A lily. To treasure the gold chain with the diamond cross. Not to hold it too often, so that the touch of his mother's hand when she gave it to Matangi-Ma would stay on it.

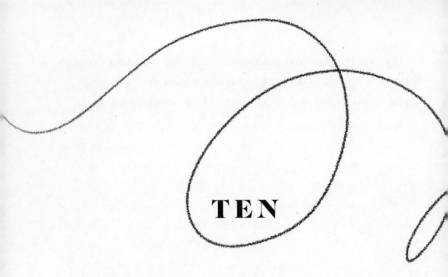

TEN

Samir had bookmarked a few websites for the family tree he was helping Rahul with. They did a trial paper run, drawing out an actual tree on the blank reverse side of the March page of the Compass International calendar.

It began with Matangi-Ma and her husband, their grandfather Prabodh Kumar Sharma. Rahul had an old Compass diary on which he wrote down the queries. He could have done this on his computer but it seemed more serious, more like a 'project', to be taking notes like this.

There was a question mark over Matangi-Ma's parents and a similar query about P.K. Sharma's parents. The first task was to search names and photographs of these unknowns.

The chart then extended to their children, Suryaveer, Shanta and Satish. Suryaveer devolved into Samir. There was some discussion about whether to include Trump's name below Shanta's. Samir pointed out that they would have to include Dollar, in which case they would have to include the turtle that Rahul had as a pet before Ritika insisted he gift it to a friend who lived in a farmhouse.

'I guess Dollar and Trump could be in a separate subset, like cousins?'

'You are smart, young Rahul!' Samir said approvingly.

Rahul's other grandmother, Kaveri, was placed above Ritika along with a question mark over his maternal grandfather's name.

Samir took the green felt marker from Rahul and pointed two arrows above his own name. He wrote out the letters with care, his eyes lit up with joyous concentration: 'Aditya Sharan Jha, Samira Susan.'

Rahul observed Samir, his mood, his intensity. He was consumed by curiosity but he knew this was not the moment to ask questions. They were working on this project together, they would search the questions and seek the answers together.

The immediate task was to gather the dates of birth and, where relevant, the dates of death (D.O.B. and D.O.D) of the people whose names they had scrolled out on the calendar paper. There were names missing—Matangi's parents, her husband's parents, Ritika's father. This was Task I.

Task II was to collect (Samir called it collate) photographs and any memorabilia around the persons listed in the chart.

Task III was to put it all together (Samir called it compile) and take the project forward.

Rahul was in charge of speaking to Matangi-Ma and his mother Ritika, to 'compile and collate' the information. He set off, full of determination and purpose.

Samir looked at the photograph of his mother. 'Time I started searching for my dad too, Mum,' he said to her. 'The lockdown as a time of discovery. Samir Sharma Susan Jha. What a mouthful!'

Rahul went to Matangi-Ma for help. She was forthcoming but not communicative. 'My father's name? Matang Singh Kashyap. He died on 15 August 1950. He was forty-five years old at the time. Subtract forty-five from 1950 and you will know when he was born. My mother? She was named Lalita. Lalita Kashyap. She was a Sharma before she got married. As I became after I got married. Shanta has photographs. I will tell her to share some with you.'

He tried to interrogate his mother. Ritika volunteered her father's name. Arvind Kumar Gaur. She would check on his date of birth—he died the year after she got married, three years before Rahul was born. And yes, she would find the photographs, they were in an album somewhere. She was coping with too much at the moment, she said to Rahul, a plea in her voice. She would get him all the information she needed, she just needed some time.

The tragedy in Bollywood had shaken everyone up. Irrfan Khan had died at the height of his cinematic career. The death of Indian cinema's most beloved actor hit everyone in different ways. Ritika was heartbroken at having lost the happy-go-lucky poet of *Qarib Qarib Singlle*. She would have shared her water bottle with him anytime, and now he was gone. For Satish, it was Raj Batra of *Hindi Medium*. It also mattered to him as an accountant that it had been one of the highest-grossing films in the worldwide box office.

Suryaveer didn't watch films or television. Samir was lost in his own world, and the news scarcely touched him. It was Shanta who felt the pain the most. She had watched all his films, from *Maqbool* to *Lunchbox* to *Haider*. The two men with whom she had been almost in love both had a look of Irrfan Khan. Mazhar Bakht had the same liquid eyes, set in a face marked by its ordinariness. Ravi Menon had looked like Irrfan too, with his lean physique, his curly hair and the keen attention with which he observed life.

Self-effacing Irrfan Khan, straddling Bollywood and Hollywood, had died of cancer, not the virus. His death seemed to reflect the panic of the times. It was the death of a dream. It confirmed to Shanta that she was destined to be a spinster forever. A lonely single woman with a beautiful cat and a kitchen where something was always on the boil.

Irrfan's death had alerted her, as it had his legions of fans, that they were losing the battle with life. Some will, some agency, was being wrested from them all as India cowered at home for the storm to pass.

Before the lockdown, before the virus had frightened the world into submission, before it had leapt out of China to wreak its havoc, before all that, Shanta had a busy, stimulating life. She worked full hours with Women for Peace. She travelled constantly, to Rwanda, to Copenhagen, to Belarus, to Mumbai, to Chennai, to Uttarakhand. She complained about the traffic in the city. She was always on the edge of burnout, and the coffee and the jetlag and the nervous energy that consumed her was also what had sustained her.

Now, deep into total lockdown, she felt panic and despair. There were the containment zones, the interstate boundaries, the mandatory health app that would rob her, and everyone she knew and all those she didn't know, of their privacy. And who were these people, in India, in America, in China, in Russia, who had seized the stage? Who, what, had allowed them to get away with it?

This was beyond capitalism, beyond class, beyond the spaces of the right and the left. This was more like the fairy tales of her childhood, of the Ice Queen, or of ogres and sleeping princesses. This was about capture, submission and stagnation, about selfhood and the loss of agency. A spell had been cast, on the poor and the rich, the ill and the well. Who would break the spell, and how?

Not by cooking more and more meals for more and more poor. Not by wearing a mask and being afraid to breathe. This forced incarceration was a test, at so many levels, of so many things.

She cuddled Trump as she stared blankly at the news, but her mood communicated itself to the cat. Miss Trump bristled and hissed and gave her a contemptuous stare before leaping into the garden.

Defeated, Shanta tried to console herself in the kitchen, cooking a caramel custard for her brother Surya and nephew Samir. But the milk curdled, and the carton of eggs fell to the floor, making a mess which she tried helplessly to clean up until Munni came to her rescue.

The omens were not good. But there was no option but to carry on. She would stay at her post and continue her fight. She would go up to her mother's flat, seek shelter in her calm, clear presence.

Her mother, Lali and Pappoo were gathered around the small table by the window. Surya was there too. The brass birdcage had been cleaned and polished and placed on the table. The bird was perched on the hoop, staring solemnly at the ring of faces around. It let out a loud sharp cry to welcome her. Surya was holding a notebook in his hand. He gestured to Shanta to join them.

'I was reciting some poems to Matangi-Ma,' he said. Some bird poems I had jotted for her. I read Keats for her, the *Ode to a Nightingale*. And Shelley, *To a Skylark*. Listen to this now, in Hindi.'

He cleared his throat and began: '*Pakshi aur Badal* by Ramdhari Singh Dinkar.'

He read out the evocative poem on birds and their travels, addressing it to the bird in the cage. 'Do you understand, little barbet?' he asked tenderly. 'One day you too will be free to fly the sky, to the clouds. When you have healed.'

Their mother nodded. Shanta found she had tears in her eyes. Suryaveer and his poems—he hadn't changed at all!

But he hadn't finished yet. 'A few lines from *Hamlet*,' he declared. 'There is a special providence in the fall of a sparrow. If it be now, 'tis not to come; if it be not to come, it will be now; if it be not now, yet it will come—the readiness is all.'

Matangi had paid no attention to Shakespeare and *Hamlet*. Shanta could make no sense of the lines and gave up on them. Suryaveer left them with a bow and a flourish, making a little flying movement as he stepped out. Would he never grow up?

'I'm really upset by Irrfan Khan's death,' Shanta blurted out to her mother. 'I had only known him through his films, but I feel as though I've lost a member of my family. I haven't felt so low for years. This pandemic, people dying, being locked up in this building, and now Irrfan!'

'Stop feeling sorry for yourself,' Matangi replied in an impatient tone. 'You young people are all the same, always feeling sorry for yourself about this or that.'

Shanta was taken aback by her response and fell silent. What had come over Mummy?

'Look at me,' Matangi continued. There was an accusatory note in her voice that Shanta had never heard before. 'Look at me. I have been a good wife, a good mother, but what has life ever given me? It's given me darkness, it's left me blind. I'm stuck here, all alone, awaiting my end. Did I deserve this? No! Do I wish I had lived some more, known some more, experienced some more? Yes!'

Shanta fell silent. She wanted to weep. How much hurt, how much pent-up pain, Matangi-Ma must be carrying within her. Yet all of them, her loving children, herself included, expected her to be perpetually sane, reasonable and kind—the all-forgiving mother who had nurtured and guided them all their lives.

'I never got to see any of Irrfan's films!' Matangi continued bitterly. 'So while all of you are weeping for him, I find I am weeping for myself! My end is coming, I can see it is, and I wonder, what was it all about? Is that all there was to it?'

Shanta was stricken. She wanted to hug her mother, to cover her with kisses, but she knew this was not the moment. Matangi-Ma was as stressed as anyone else. The cracks were showing up. Her mother needed distraction, not a demonstration of affection.

'Let's watch Irrfan's films together,' she said brightly. 'Let me search for *Lunchbox* or *Maqbool*. You can listen to the dialogues and I will fill in the blanks for you.'

So they settled down to a session of artistic consolation, with the bird chirping occasionally in the background to assert its presence.

ELEVEN

The Western disturbances were playing around with the weather, as they often did at this time of the year. It was sometimes sunny, sometimes rainy and windy.

The red cotton tree was shedding its wispy pods of semal. They settled on Matangi's veranda, Ritika's balcony, Shanta's garden. 'They look like snow!' said Rahul, who had never seen snow.

Ritika nodded her head in weary agreement. The floating semal seeds had provoked her annual bout of hay fever, and she was on a heavy dose of self-prescribed anti-allergens. Satish had gone over to the chemist wearing a surgical mask and gloves to buy the medicine for her.

Rahul had collected the elusive wisps of semal cotton and piled them up in a heap on the dining table. Never in his life had he seen anything so enticing. He was contemplating the mound of cotton 'snow' when Ritika walked in. The anti-allergens had left her disoriented, and although she had been lying in bed the last few days, restful sleep had eluded her.

Rahul had been waiting to share the triumph of his accumulated treasure with his parents. He held a handful of the snow in his palm and playfully blew it towards his mother. It was a loving gesture, and her reaction took him completely by surprise.

Ritika felt the cottony semal land on her face and her hair as Rahul blew them in her direction. All the anger, the anxiety, the discomfort of the past month rose inside her like a torrent. She lost control.

Rahul found himself grabbed by his hair and lifted up. His mother was shaking him violently, this way and that, before she threw him to the ground. He watched her as she went to the dining table, picked up the remaining balls of snow and heaped them over her head.

'You want your mother to die? You want me to die, don't you?' she screamed. 'Why not just go and collect some coronavirus instead and spit it into my face? What have I done to deserve this?'

Her meltdown was complete. She sat down on the floor, weeping hysterically.

Satish had walked in halfway through the drama. He reached out and held his son close to him.

'What has gone wrong with you, Ritika?' he exclaimed in dismay. 'I will not let this young child stay under the same roof as you until you get yourself in order. You will apologize to him now and to me later.'

He brought her a glass of water. 'Drink this,' he said. 'No more of the anti-anxiety pills you have been devouring. Get a hold of yourself. Or else . . .'

Rahul was shaking uncontrollably. His eyes were full of tears but he couldn't weep. He set about collecting the scattered wisps of snow and piling them up on the table. He was waiting for his mother to apologize to him, to take him in her arms and hug him, to explain.

But she didn't. She had gone to her room and locked the door.

'Go pack your nightclothes and a toothbrush, Rahul,' Satish said to him gently. 'You will stay in your grandmother's flat tonight. Matangi-Ma will be so delighted to spend time with you.'

Rahul did as he was told. He took the snow with him, safe in a plastic bag, and a book to read. He cast a cautious, anxious look towards his mother's bedroom and tiptoed out.

Satish walked up with him to the floor above. 'You have a visitor, Matangi-Ma,' he said cheerfully. 'Your grandson is bored of the lockdown. He wants to spend time with you.'

'Switch off the television,' Matangi instructed Lali. 'I want to tell Rahul a story today.'

But Lali was glued to the television. Rishi Kapoor had died. The news channel had begun on a clip from his first film, *Bobby*, followed by a tearful shraddhanjali and celebrity condolences. Matangi had been in her thirties when she saw the film, in a cinema hall with her friends. She used to wear spectacles those days. She had fallen in love with him, and with his girlfriend Bobby too. She had hated his rich parents, and rather despised Dimple Kapadia's fisherman father as well.

Rishi Kapoor, son of Raj Kapoor, grandson of Prithviraj Kapoor. He was, had been, Bollywood royalty, and she paid obeisance in her heart. First Irrfan, now Rishi. Why were they dying so young, these boys? Why had Yamdoot, the lord of death, decided to abduct the chocolate boy of Bollywood?

She felt an enormous guilt descend upon her, the weight of being alive. Here she was, at eighty, blind as a bat, of no particular use to anyone. A burden upon her loving children. And it was the young who were dying.

'Did Rishi Kapoor die of the coronavirus, Matangi-Ma?' Rahul asked her.

'No, beta, he did not die of the virus. He died of . . .' She bit her tongue. Why frighten a little boy with the spectre of cancer? 'Rishi Kapoor didn't die of Covid. He died because God wanted him in heaven, to make a Bollywood film there.'

Of course, the child wouldn't believe her, but her answer would divert him, she thought.

But the idea appealed to Rahul. He nodded enthusiastically. 'That's why Irrfan Khan was called up. I wonder who God will cast next, for the female lead?'

Rahul had brought the precious bag of squashed semal pods with him. He shared the cotton wisps with Matangi excitedly flinging them around her bed and watching them flurry down. She told him he was the cleverest boy in the world. She would make herself a tiny pillow from the semal cotton, she said, a special pillow that would give her beautiful dreams.

Matangi uttered a silent prayer, a plea without words that rose from the depth of her heart. It was addressed to anybody who might be listening—to the gods, the goddesses, to Yamdoot, to Rishi Kapoor if he was hovering around.

'Let me die now,' she prayed. 'Let me gift my remaining years to this beloved boy. May he live to be a hundred years, or more. But take me away. I have lived enough.'

They spent a delightful day together—Lali and Pappoo and Rahul and Matangi and the bird. They played absurd games, games which made no sense, but which made them laugh. Lali made mango milkshake for all of them, for Matangi too.

Does the bird have a name, Rahul had asked, and they discovered to their surprise that nobody had named it yet.

'Mithoo,' Lali had suggested. Pappoo had amended that to 'Mithoo Mian'. Matangi suggested 'Mirchi'. Rahul had to think hard before he came up with 'Captain Covid'.

They agreed on 'Mirchi' as Matangi was the oldest among them, and had discovered the bird, saved it from being eaten by the black cat that had been waiting in the shadows.

Besides, as Matangi explained, 'Mirchi' would work equally well for a boy bird or a girl bird, and the barbet's gender was still of course a mystery.

Rahul didn't think about his mother or about all that had happened earlier in the day. He read out the poem he had written, the one about the lockdown, to his grandmother, and she was suitably impressed. He changed into his night suit later and slept on a mattress on the floor, which was fun. Lali and Pappoo and the bird slept in the veranda, as usual.

The next morning, Ritika went upstairs to Matangi's floor to talk to Rahul, to apologize to him for her behaviour. She was still shaken up by all that had passed the previous night. She had slept alone, as Satish had taken his pillow from their bedroom and camped on the living-room couch.

Matangi was dozing in her bed, her face to the wall. Rahul was sitting by the small table by the window, reading a book. There was large brass cage on the table, with an odd-looking bird in it.

Rahul smiled when he saw her. 'Hullo, Mummy!' he said. 'Meet Mirchi, my new friend. Matangi-Ma has magical powers and saved Mirchi's life.'

Ritika was cut off from the gossip circuit in the building. She had not heard of the mysterious discovery of the bird and dismissed Rahul's words as childish prattle. She was in any case too absorbed in rehearsing the formal apology she intended to make to her son.

But there was no need. Rahul put his book away, marking the page he was on, and rushed forward to hug her. 'Don't bother about yesterday, Mummy,' he said. 'Grown-ups can have problems too, just like children. I'm old enough to understand that.'

She broke down. He hugged her, consoled her, stroked her hair with his little hands.

Matangi heard her soft sobs. She turned over questioningly. 'Who is that crying, Rahul? I can hear someone crying.'

Ritika went over and sat down near her mother-in-law. 'It's me, Matangi-Ma,' she said, trying but failing to control her tears.

Matangi sat up on her bed and reached out to stroke Ritika's face. She encountered the tears streaming down, but said nothing. 'Don't worry, Rinku,' she said gently. 'Everything will be all right. You may think your world is falling apart, but it's not. You will get some good news, today or tomorrow, and you will soon be sitting here, smiling. No more tears, Rinku!'

Ritika was dumbfounded. Matangi had called her Rinku! That had been her pet name when she was a child. Her mother would call her Rinku, until she was twelve or perhaps thirteen. Nobody knew her as Rinku any more. Her father was dead and her mother lived in her own muddled mental world. She had never mentioned it even to Satish. Why had her mother-in-law addressed her with that forgotten endearment? How did she know?

Matangi was reading some lines from a poem now.

Saubhagya na har din sota hai . . .
Dekho aage kya hota hai?

She turned to Ritika with her sightless eyes. 'Even the Pandavas had to wander in exile, as did Rama and Sita. Difficult days are inevitable, but I bless you, my only daughter-in-law, with all the good fortune in the world. Now wipe away those tears.'

'Why did you call me Rinku, Matangi-Ma?' Ritika asked her eagerly.

Matangi tugged at her ear. She looked puzzled. 'Did I?' she asked confusedly.

Ritika bent down to touch her feet. 'Thank you for your blessings,' she said. 'I shall value them all my life.'

The Blind Matriarch

Rahul had been watching them wide-eyed. He pulled at Ritika's dupatta. 'Let's go home now, Mummy,' he said. 'It's time to go home.'

Her husband materialized in her dream. His twitching moustache. The smell of his hair oil.

In her dream, she had confronted him. She couldn't remember what she had said, but she had mocked him, challenged him.

He slapped her. She didn't slap him back. She left the room, afraid of violence. The memory of that slap remained imprinted on her cheek long after she awoke.

Satish was in his study, engrossed in a Zoom call. Rahul returned to his room to watch a film. The day passed peacefully. In the afternoon, Ritika received a phone call from her domestic help. The nearby cluster of slums had been marked a containment zone. Irina needed to send money to her mother in Jharkhand. Would Ritika loan her an advance of ten thousand rupees, perhaps help have it transferred to her village? Her mother had an account with the State Bank of India. Irina would pay it off, once she got back to work.

Ritika had decided to go tight on her budget, contain all extra costs. Irina was an erratic worker; she hadn't been with her for long. But something about her voice, when she said her mother needed the money, made her pause. They were all in it together. Her mother, Irina's mother, Satish's mother.

'I will send her the money,' she said. 'WhatsApp me the details.'

She went to her balcony for a smoke. The evening was beginning to settle in. The mosaic floor was covered with fallen sheuli blossoms. The tiny flowers, trampled by the wind, gave off their elusive fragrance. There had been a parijat tree in the garden of the house where she grew up. Her mother would step out to tenderly gather up the night flowers at dawn, just after they had fallen to the floor.

Her mother would make a decoction of the sheuli flowers. The sweet-smelling pottage tasted bitter and she could never be persuaded to have it.

'But what is it for?' she would ask. Her mother would never give her a straight reply. She would launch into some story instead, usually about Krishna. She told Ritika about how Radha and Krishna would be covered with parijat flowers when they awoke together at dawn in the woods of Vrindavan. She told her of Krishna's wives, Satyabhama and Rukmini. Lord Indra had gifted Krishna a parijat tree, and proud Satyabhama had insisted it be planted in her courtyard. But the tree would bend its branches at night and shower its fragrant gifts into Rukmini's garden.

'There is a lesson there, Ritika,' she told her daughter. 'Life doesn't yield its gifts simply because you demand them. You have to be patient, to be able to give things away, and they will come to you in abundance.'

The cigarette smoke had cleared Ritika's head. She hadn't run through the cache of ultra-slim cigarettes in her cupboard yet. Her outburst, her unravelling of the day before, had left her tired and bewildered. Her conversation with her mother-in-law had soothed her, had calmed her down, in a visceral way.

Rahul had told her the story of the bird, how Matangi-Ma had rescued it with her second sight. Ritika was sure the tale was embellished by Lali's fanciful exaggerations but there was something about the old lady. Something of another world. She couldn't deny that.

Why had she called her Rinku? She seemed vague about it later, perhaps it was just a vestigial memory from some forgotten conversation. Perhaps her mother had mentioned it to Matangi-Ma the only time they had met.

Her mother. She had wanted to name her Sheuli, after the flower of the sacred parijat tree. Her parents had settled for Ritika instead, for her father found it pointless to name her for a flower that bloomed for one brief night.

She inhaled the fragrance again. The parijat tree never caused her any allergies. Perhaps she could still change her name. Sheuli Sharma. Life was full of infinite possibilities. Sheuli Ritika Sharma, so she wouldn't need to change her bank account or her passport.

She sighed. The holes in her bank account were already showing up. And as for passports, there wasn't any use for them in the brave new world.

Her phone rang. It was her boss, Girish Syal. She took the call, both curious and apprehensive.

'I have some news for you, Ritika,' he said. 'I've had a stroke of luck, which puts Compass International in the clear for a while. I received some old outstanding payments, which I had all but written off. The world will land on its feet, and so will we.'

'We?' she wondered warily.

'And my brother-in-law has put me on to a major digital project. It's early days still, but there's the potential to make a killing. So I'd like you to get back to work, with me. I appreciate you didn't jump ship when things went wrong, but offered to stand by Compass International. We will swim to the shore, yes we will, if we are lucky. So, there is a position for you here, Ritika, if you would like to take it on. A reasonable fee to begin with, and work from home, but we can ride the wave on this. I know we can.'

'I'm on,' she said. 'We are in it together. When do we begin?'

She took a deep breath and lit up another cigarette. Matangi-Ma's blessing. She could go on paying her bills, feeling in charge of her own life.

It was strange, Ritika reflected, how financial insecurity panned out. She had never actually been short of money in her life. Satish could provide for her and more. Her mother had tried to pamper Ritika, to get her the things young girls wanted—new clothes, shoes, perfume. But her father had been mean and miserly.

'I work for a public sector undertaking,' he had told his daughter. 'Not like those private sector fellows. I can give you the essentials. You can indulge yourself all you want after you are married off.'

Her arranged marriage with Satish had come through the matrimonial pages of the *Times of India*. 'Brahmin boy from educated family with accounting background seeks tall, broad-minded and well-brought-up girl.' She was unprepared for the family she married into. She couldn't understand Shanta and could fathom Surya even less. Her sightless mother-in-law terrified her.

Satish was kind to her, but she did not feel at ease with her new family. She couldn't decode their jokes, understand the unwritten rules. Her husband, always careful about money, had given her a ledger the day after they were married and asked her to write a detailed account of all that she spent. It was only after she got a job that she came into her own. It was as though a blank hole in her identity, a vacuum in her selfhood, had filled up.

Ritika thought again of the old lady, of her prescient if garbled blessing. A song from her college days rose to her lips. 'Oh no, not I, I will survive,' she hummed, struggling to remember the rest of the words.

The Blind Matriarch

She sensed a presence in the veranda above. It was her mother-in-law, taking in the evening breeze. She was singing, too, in a wheezy voice. The words were indistinct and the melody plaintive—it could have been a bhajan or a filmi love song.

Ritika looked up at her and smiled. She stubbed out her cigarette. 'You are a survivor, Rinku,' she told herself, as she blew a kiss towards the shadowy figure of Matangi on the floor above.

Upstairs, Matangi was feeling low and dispirited. The dream visitation from her departed husband had unsettled her. She could still smell the reek of his hair oil, recall the sneer in his face. She could remember it all, before she had decided not to see.

She had applied for a job once, to teach craft in the nursery classes in a nearby Sarvodaya Vidyalaya. It was a temporary job, so they had bypassed the need for a B.Ed. degree. He had scoffed at her when she applied, been contemptuous when she got it. 'You will just be a glorified ayah,' he had said. 'They gave you the job because your husband is a senior government servant. They don't realize that you are going blind!'

She went to work for a week, dressed in crisp cotton saris, blinking through her thick glasses, until he forbade her from continuing. She had defied him, refused to resign, to give up so easily, to submit to him again. Until the accident.

She had forgotten her art file and returned after class was over to get it. The sweeperess had been pouring phenyl into a steel bucket when Matangi tripped over it. She fell to the floor, and the bottle of phenyl slipped from the cleaner's hand, spilling over her. The burning liquid splashed over her face, her eyes, her mouth. She remembered the acrid taste in her mouth, and her eyes, consumed by icy fire.

113

The principal's office had called her husband and he had come to pick her up. People had gathered around her; they washed her eyes with water, but that had only made it worse.

'I told you that you are unfit to hold a job,' he had told her, when he saw her, wet, dishevelled, shattered. By the time she reached home, she had lost her vision, completely and forever.

She had visited doctors in the eye hospital, her husband had made sure of that and accompanied her. The doctors tutted in concern and made her undergo endless tests. She could make out if a light was switched on, or off, when it was shone in her eyes, but that was all.

'The chemical burns from liquid cleaner cannot make you blind,' the doctor had said, kindly but firmly. 'There was already an existing precondition of wet macular degeneration, which we had warned you about; but to have lost all your vision—even your peripheral vision—I cannot understand it. It may be emotional trauma—or . . .'

'Her husband had been in a hurry to leave. There was an important meeting that afternoon, and his boss had asked for some papers. He had left her in the hospital, with the doctors. 'You can go home alone,' he had said. 'Doctor Saheb, see that your chaprasi gets her into a taxi.'

She remembered little of that clattering drive home. She had whimpered with pain and humiliation, and resolved never to see his face again. The doctor had called her back, puzzled over her. But she still could not see. Or she would not see.

The school was informed that she would not be returning. The children in her class had sent her a card. She had felt the texture of the crayons, of the poster colours, the glue. She thought she could see the colours, the warmth and glow in them, but perhaps she was imagining it. She had willed herself to darkness.

'Enough', she told herself firmly, returning to the present. 'Forget the dead. Nurture the living.'

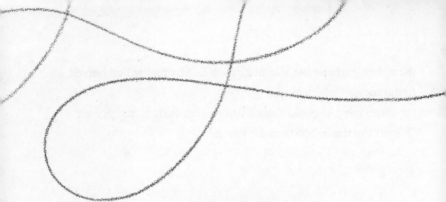

TWELVE

Suryaveer kept a watchful eye on Samir, but he was for the most part consumed by his book, which had been a work-in-progress for many years now. He was attempting to untangle the constant conflict of ideas playing around in his restless mind. While researching the old volumes in his library, he came across a copy of *Lokayata*, the timeless classic by Debiprasad Chattopadhyay. The tattered paperback edition stood at the very highest corner of the bookshelf, its broken spine making it all but invisible.

He extracted it carefully, even tenderly, from the shelf. It was an early edition, published by People's Publishing House. Surya's eyes misted over as he held it in his hands. This book, more than any other, had awakened him to the puzzles and anomalies of the culture he inhabited. He had argued with this book, agreed with it, learnt from it, forgotten it.

The front page carried his name, in bold black ink, still unfaded with the passage of years: 'Suryaveer—from Aniruddha'. The familiar handwriting awakened all sorts of emotions within him. He could almost see Aniruddha before him, here, now. They had been roommates in hostel. Their perpetually disorderly room was always piled high with books. Aniruddha had picked it up from a heap of newspapers, periodicals and mysterious brown paper envelopes and handed it over with a smile.

Aniruddha. Aditya's brother. Samir's paternal uncle, his chacha. Where was Aniruddha now? Was he still alive?

There had been a bitter falling out the last time that they met. Aniruddha had demanded that Suryaveer rescind the adoption papers, give up Samir, return him to the Jha family. Matangi and Suryaveer had already been given joint custody of the child. Aniruddha had threatened to contest the matter in court.

Samira's parents were in frail health. Their daughter's death had left them distraught, but they were reconciled to her decision to leave her only child in Suryaveer's care. They had left a will, with a trust fund in Samir's name, to be given to him when he turned twenty-two.

These were all things Surya meant to share with Samir, but the boy was not yet ready. He was still processing the hurt, the sense of loss, that had arisen when he learnt of his true parentage. Surya would tell him all this, and more, when he was ready.

'Don't ever give my child up to Aditya's family,' Samira had implored him. 'They threw their son out, broke off with him, because he married me, because I'm a Christian. Not a Hindu, not a Bihari, not a Brahmin, but a Mangalorean Christian. They are primitive, barbaric patriarchs. I don't want them to have any rights over my son.'

Aniruddha had made the contrary argument. 'Samira snatched my brother away, stole him from our family. He would be alive today if he hadn't got caught up with her hare-brained revolutionary ideas. Now my brilliant brother is dead. Samira is dead. I want my nephew back, my parents want him back. He is our blood. You can't deny that.'

'I gave Samira my word,' Suryaveer replied steadfastly. 'I made a promise to a woman I respected.'

He had admired Samira for her stubborn strength. He had been dazzled by her, perhaps even been a little in love with her.

117

She had an incandescent quality, of liquid fire. And of course he had loved Aditya, as a brother, as more than a brother.

'Blood is thicker than water,' Aniruddha had said. 'The boy will return to us one day. I know you will look after him well, Surya. I trust you, but I will not forgive you, ever, for this high-minded stubbornness.'

In *Lokayata: A Study in Ancient Indian Materialism*, Debiprasad Chattopadhyay reconstructed the other forgotten philosophical traditions of India. The book had been an eye-opener for the young Suryaveer, opening up so many avenues of reflection and doubt.

Ah well. The past was the past. Suryaveer returned to his notes. 'Of the many categories of learning, the Lokayata (Sanskrit: the worldly ones), also known as the Charvaka, recognized only that of "anubhav", or direct perception.' He examined the lines and they seemed opaque, as though they belonged precisely to the sort of book he didn't want or intend to write.

He tried to get down to it again. 'The fuzzy, woolly-headed perception of what might be loosely called the Hindu religion as central to Indian philosophy comes from the purposeful amnesia regarding other schools of thought, which persist in their shadows even today in almost every aspect of material life in the subcontinent.'

He scratched out 'subcontinent' and replaced it with 'South Asia'. He objected to both classifications for different reasons, and changed it around again: '. . . in almost every aspect of the lived material life in what might be described as the Indian civilizational culture.'

But his mind was still on Aniruddha. It was as though he had leapt out of the black ink inscription of the book he had gifted Suryaveer so many years ago. It was time to tell Samir, to show him the book with his uncle Aniruddha's handwriting, to tell him of how his father's brother had quarrelled with Surya to get him back.

Surya had loved Samir unconditionally from the day Samira had handed him over. Perhaps it was the selfish fear of losing him to his father's family that had kept him silent on his true parentage. He had wondered, often, why the boy showed so little curiosity about his roots and his birth parents. Perhaps he had been afraid, too, of what he might discover.

Well, Samir had come of age now. He was secure in his identity as Samir Sharma, as Surya's son and Matangi's grandson. It would all end well, it surely would.

Although Samir's enthusiasm for the drums had waned considerably, he was practising on them that afternoon. What else was there to do in the days of the lockdown? He had watched *Pandemic* twice, back to back. He had watched *Panchayat* and even persuaded Suryaveer to watch it with him. They had both admired Jitendra Kumar's acting, and Surya told him of his longstanding crush on Neena Gupta, which seemed incomprehensible to Samir.

Surya walked into Samir's room, casually holding the book in his hand. He didn't say much at first, just stroked Dollar and removed a tick from his ear, which he then flushed down the toilet.

He sat in silence for a while, nodding his head appreciatively in time to the beat. 'Your father had a brother,' he said finally, quite out of the blue. 'An elder brother, Aniruddha Sharan Jha. I thought I would tell you about him.'

Samir raised an eyebrow and continued with his desultory drumming, stopping occasionally to push back the long hair that kept falling over his face. He hadn't had a haircut since the lockdown began.

'I haven't forgiven my father,' Samir said at last. 'It was irresponsible of him to cast me away as he did. My mother . . . Samira . . .' His voice took on a tender note when he said her name. 'She is reaching out across time to me. I can feel her love, her concern. But that dude, I can't bring myself to forgive him. There's a missing link there somewhere. And his family never bothered to lay claim to me, did they? So, why would I bother if my father, my birth father, had a brother called Aniruddha?'

This was followed by a furious burst of drumming. Munni rang at the doorbell and left a jug of mango milkshake and a banana cake in the dining room.

'I'm hungry,' said Samir, slurping down the mango milkshake before he went for the banana cake.

'Your uncle Aniruddha and I quarrelled bitterly over your custody,' Suryaveer said gently, as he played around with the crumbs of banana cake on the dining table. 'He told me that you would return to the family someday, that blood was thicker than water. I was looking for a reference book and came across this old copy of *Lokayata*, which Aniruddha had gifted me.'

Samir got up with a decisive movement. The chair he was sitting on overturned, and he positioned it back carefully.

'I need a smoke,' he said, and returned to his room. He emerged wearing a face mask and sneakers. Dollar followed him out.

The park was looking tidier today, better tended. One of the neighbours jogged past him, huffing and puffing under his surgical mask. The days had gotten longer, although the scorching temperatures of May had mysteriously not manifested this year. The grass was overgrown but still green, and some flowers remained in bloom—withered impatiens and a bed of hollyhocks that were drooping dispiritedly to the ground.

Samir settled down on a bench in a deserted corner of the park and lit up. He had found a joint lying beside the half-empty pack of cigarettes in his room. He was not really a smoker, and only an occasional drinker. The hand-rolled spliff had been left behind in his cupboard by a friend who had come to stay, before the days of the lockdown.

He felt calmer and more relaxed. His mind was purposefully blank, as empty and reflective as his surroundings. It was as though he had stepped through an invisible door to the other side, another world where everything was the same but not quite.

There was a movement in the grass. The green blades were swaying to an undulating dance. Samir thought he was hallucinating.

A pair of glassy eyes were examining him intently. A snake? He felt no fear. The joint had left him peaceable, accepting. He watched the snake as it watched him.

Samir had no idea how long he sat there. The late afternoon sun had tinted to the mellower shades of evening. The snake had slithered away towards the children's area, where the swings were. Dollar came and pulled at his shorts, barking and urging him to return home.

That night he had a headache and felt sick. But something had recalibrated within him. He didn't need to play the drums any more. He wasn't angry with his father, with Aditya Sharan Jha. The hurt had leached out of him during his long afternoon in the park, with the emerald green snake observing him from the grass.

Surya had lost count of the hours. He was immersed in re-reading Debiprasad Chattopadhyay's classic, which had first alerted him to so many conflicting perspectives and ways of seeing.

Historical materialism and the inspired glimpse into the origins of Hindu ritual practice had provided a radical reorientation to Surya's largely savarna upper-caste understanding of his religion. He had always been drawn to poetry and mysticism, but *Lokayata* has sharpened his gaze and understanding beyond his naive and rather woolly assumptions. His friendship with Aniruddha, and later with his brother Aditya, had led him to take an exhilarating leap into the radical politics of the left.

He was lost now in the dense prose and the constantly accelerating play of ideas, busily taking notes in his lined notebook. 'DP views the movement of Indian philosophy as the interplay of a real conflict of ideas,' he noted, 'with contradiction constituting the moving force behind Indian philosophical development.'

But another part of his mind kept returning to Aniruddha. Should he have opened that front with Samir? Would it have been better to wait awhile before telling him?

Upstairs, Matangi was listening to the *Mahabharat* episodes playing on Doordarshan. The rousing title song, the long-drawn-out Maha-aa-bha-aa-rat, had reintroduced India to the epic in those early days of colour television.

Her mind went back to 1988. Satish must have been five, and Surya just entering his teens. They would all cluster around the television in the drawing-cum-dining room in Kaka Nagar. Shanta couldn't be bothered to watch the show with them. 'It's just too boring and unreal,' she would say, rolling her eyes. 'Give me a break, family.'

Not that she could see Shanta rolling her eyes. Her sight was deteriorating, every day, every moment. Macular degeneration with retinal complications. She could still hear the doctor's indifferent voice when he told her it was irreversible and she would have to learn to live with it.

1988. 2020. Blindness. Darkness. Listening to the dialogue in the revived mythic tele-drama was like a visceral hurt, a stab in the heart. King Dhritarashtra, son of Ambika and Vichitravirya, was born blind. He married Gandhari, the princess of Kandahar, who gave up her sight after marriage, voluntarily blindfolding herself.

The words flew out like arrows from the direction of the screen. *Netra-heen. Andhkaar.* Lacking sight. Living in darkness. Her blindness had come to her gradually and the memory of sight had lingered. She had been bitter yet resigned. Through the years, she had become reconciled to the reality of her life, its compensatory joys, until the remembered dialogue from an old serial jumped out of the television to accost and wound her.

The lockdown was exhausting her, although it had changed nothing in her routine. Everything was the same as it had ever been, the hourly cheeps of the cuckoo clock, the barbet's insistent too-hay-too-hay, the sounds of the television, Pappoo running his imaginary car in the veranda, VRROOM VRROOOM. Everything was as it had been, but there was another unheard sound, a sense of monotonous expectancy, a fear, a waiting without end. She could hear it in her children's voices when they asked her how she was feeling. She could hear it in Lali's tense, whispered conversations with her family. She could hear it in the news, of migrant labour being run over by trains, of ordinary people being crushed to death by trucks as they tried to make their way home.

Matangi was feeling uncharacteristically sorry for herself and for the world, when Samir arrived upstairs to chat with her. His voice had a tremor to it, and she could sense that he was intensely disturbed about something. 'How did you hear the bird, Matangi-Ma?' he asked her.

She considered his question for a long while. 'There are many windows to the body,' she said finally. 'The facial orifices—your two eyes, two nostrils, your mouth. And then there are our two ears, and the two holes below for women.'

123

She indicated this as delicately as she could. 'We rely too much on our vision. I've only lost the sight in my two eyes, but I have been gifted other things. I have sound and smell beyond what I had before.' My taste buds have remained the same, which is just as well; I would always be complaining to Shanta about this or that in her cooking. And sometimes the gods and goddesses come and whisper in my ears. So, I heard that bird as clearly as I can hear it now. It was speaking to me, calling to me.'

'Does it still speak to you?' Samir persisted. He felt deeply invested in the bird, and his mind kept returning to the time he had found it splayed across the pavement, with the black cat examining it with intent, preparing to pounce.

'Of course, it speaks to me,' Matangi replied. 'It tells me of its mother, and the shady tree where its nest is. It spoke to me today, and told me it was time to set it free.'

Samir's heart beat fast. 'You mean you intend to let it go?' he asked intently. 'You will let it fly away?'

'I don't believe in cages,' Matangi replied reflectively. 'I have lived in one. It's time to let it go.'

'When, Matangi-Ma? When will you set it free? Has it healed? Is it ready to fly now?'

'It has to test its wings,' she replied. 'You will take it down tomorrow and leave it on the middle branch of the tree where you found it. You will wear plastic gloves, one of your Covid ones, and wait and watch until it is safe. But first it must test its wings. Set it free now, Samir, and let it fly around the room. Now!'

He did as he was told and unlatched the door of the cage. The bird stared at the opening between the brass bars, contemplating it with blissful indifference. Samir whistled to it, made encouraging sounds, but it remained seated inside, its claws clutching firmly to the hoop.

'It doesn't want to leave the cage,' he said in despair.

'That's the way with cages; they are usually invisible for those imprisoned inside,' Matangi said, a wry smile breaking across her face.

Pappoo came crawling into the room on all fours, playing some impossible to comprehend pretend-game. Suddenly there was a flutter of wings, and the bird was out. It sat on the table and examined the scene around with beady eyes. Then it ascended the air, cautiously at first, its wings flapping asymmetrically, before it found its pace.

Samir was terrified that it would hit against the revolving blades of the ceiling fan. He rushed to switch it off, then watched wonderstruck as the barbet soared towards the ceiling.

Pappoo was wonderstruck too. He was flapping about now, pretending he was a bird, pretending he was flying. He leapt up on the chair, then leapt down. Lali gave him a smack on the face and told him to sit quietly in a corner.

The barbet had reached Matangi's bed. It circled her head, twice, then came and settled on her lap.

Lali squealed with excitement. Samir found he had tears in his eyes. Even Pappoo was quiet. Matangi sat very still, holding her breath in. She did not reach out to touch or stroke it. The bird was still too, quiet and secure. Samir felt she was speaking to it, in some silent, secret language.

'Put the bird back in its cage, Lali,' she said at last. 'We will set it free tomorrow.'

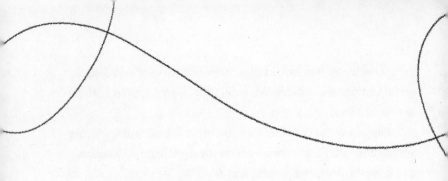

THIRTEEN

Lali arrived at the first floor with a message for Samir from Matangi. 'The bird has to be set free,' she announced. 'Mataji has said to remind you. She says she knows you wake up late these days, but she wants to send it away before noon or in the afternoon.'

'Tell her I will be upstairs by 3.45 p.m.,' Samir said sleepily. He had been up until late, looking up Aniruddha Sharan Jha, Anirudh Saran Jha, Annirudha Sharan Jha, Anirudh Sharan, Anirudh Jha, A.S. Jha and so on. There were one or two leads he meant to follow up on.

Most of the names and faces discoverable on screen were far too young to belong to his long-lost uncle. He had a mental picture of him already—a toothbrush moustache and unpleasant demeanour. A scowl.

He looked at the signature on the title page of the old book again, trying to decrypt it. It was an elegant handwriting, with a decisive swirl to the letters. What did he look like, sound like, this old man who was his blood?

The day had taken on the glazed timelessness of Covid time. Meals, sleep, the screen. In any order. He set off dutifully at 3.40 p.m. to see his grandmother as promised, messaging his cousin Rahul to join them as well. This sort of task required an assistant, he conjectured, and he didn't want the ever-garrulous Lali for that role.

Matangi was seated in the chair by the window, waiting for him. She looked even more frail than usual. The cage stood on the table before her. The bird was perched with its beak tucked into its wing, looking contemplative.

'We will carry the cage down, then, and give this fellow a taste of freedom!' Samir said cheerily.

'No!' Matangi replied sharply. 'Not like that! The cage stays here. He must forget the cage.'

'Yes, Mirchi must forget the cage, he must learn to be free,' Rahul chimed. 'Freedom is important to everybody. Rabindranath Tagore told us so.'

Pappoo was taking it all in. 'Why don't you come with us as well, young man?' Samir said to him. They set off in a strange procession, the three masked boys and the bird, down the curved staircase with the slatted brick screens in the landings. Samir thought it stupid not to carry the bird down in the cage, but his grandmother looked so fragile, so weary, that he didn't have the heart to argue with her.

'I will fly away soon too,' Matangi said as the boys stepped out. 'We all have to learn to fly away. Let the bird test its wings for a while before you send it off. The mother is waiting on the top branch of the tree.'

Samir's heart skipped a beat. What was she saying? What had she just said? He wanted to turn back, to hug her, to shake her up, to reprove her, but it would be thoughtless to make too much of her remark. Perhaps she hadn't meant it like that. Perhaps.

Samir had never encountered death, seen anyone die, except in films or video games. His parents had departed as though in a long-ago dream. He felt a sense of dread creep over him. He couldn't lose his beloved grandmother. He couldn't.

Ever. He pretended not to have registered her remark. The task of carrying Mirchi was deputed to Rahul. Pappoo followed behind him, and then Samir, in single file.

The brief season of the semal pods had passed. The red cotton tree spread its shade on the pavement. Somewhere high up on the branches, a barbet tweeped its distinctive call.

'That's Mirchi's mother,' Rahul announced gravely. 'She is waiting for her child, just as Matangi-Ma said she would be.'

Mirchi had heard the bird call. It cheeped its response and fluttered its wings eagerly.

'We have to place Mirchi in the middle branch,' Rahul said. 'But how?'

Just then, Anna Sen materialized, wearing a brightly printed cotton mask. 'You want to place the bird back on the tree?' she asked, seeming not at all surprised. 'Wait, I'll get my high stool for you.'

And there in her garden was a three-stepped wooden stool, which she dragged out with surprising ease. 'There you go!' she said. 'Samir and I will hold up the stool for you.'

Samir looked at her strangely. He had no idea that old Mrs Sen was even aware of his existence, leave alone his name.

Rahul climbed up carefully, still holding the bird in his hands. Before he was halfway up it had fluttered out of his grasp. Three barbets, green and big-beaked, had swooped down from the treetop and formed a protective cordon around it. Mirchi was home.

'Bravo!' Mrs Sen exclaimed, and clapped her hands.

Pappoo clapped his hands too, and then Samir. Rahul was quiet and pensive.

'I have a treat waiting for you,' Anna Sen continued cheerily. 'If you can bear to spend some of your valuable time with an old lady. Just wait here in the garden for a moment?'

She returned holding up an enormous tray with a jug of lemonade and slices of chocolate cake. 'You first, little one,' she said to Pappoo, chucking him under the chin. She put the tray down on the flagged path and disappeared inside again.

Rahul was still looking towards the red cotton tree, watching out for Mirchi. A chorus of birds seemed to be celebrating its return.

Anna returned with a plastic bag from which she extracted three bars of chocolate. 'These are for the three musketeers!' she declared. 'And now I leave you fine gentlemen alone, as I have some work to attend to.'

Rahul had cheered up considerably at the sight of all the chocolates. There were two flavours, plum and cherry. Samir examined them carefully. 'Polish chocolates,' he commented. 'You had better have yours here, Rahul, before your mother catches you in the act. And the same for you, Pappoo, unless you plan to share with Lali! I will share mine with Surya, and leave a bite for you, Rahul, when you come down to work on our family tree project!'

Surya had been trying to find Aniruddha, to somehow track him down. He sent messages to mutual friends, enquiring about his whereabouts. The details surfaced soon enough. Aniruddha Sharan Jha was adjunct professor of cultural anthropology at the University of Georgia. The friend had sent a number and an email address.

Surya decided to take the plunge cold. He calculated the time difference, took a deep breath, and dialled the number. There was no response. He realized he had miscalculated the time difference between India and Georgia, and decided not to leave a message.

There was a response on WhatsApp a little later. 'Received a call from this number. Who is this? A.S.J.'

He thought it through again. Samir was all he had. His family, his son, his friend. What if he were to lose Samir? It was a risk he would have to take, he decided, then dialled the number again.

'Hello? May I speak to Aniruddha Sharan Jha?' he asked hesitantly.

There was not a missed beat at the other end. '*Arre yaar*! Suryaveer . . . *Mera dost! Mera jigri dost, mere dil ka tukda*!' The outpouring of affection was in Hindi, but with the overlay of a decidedly American accent.

Surya found himself moved by the affection but annoyed by the accent. It was amazing that Aniruddha had recognized his voice so instantly, but why was he speaking Hindi in that affected way?

But there were more important things to be said. 'How are you, my friend?' he replied in English. 'Are you married? Do you have children? Are you keeping safe and in good health in these difficult times?'

'I'm fine now,' Aniruddha replied, in English this time. 'But it's been a rough year all around. My partner got Lyme Disease, which is almost unknown in these parts. It was a mystery to the doctors for the longest time before they figured it out, and then the amoxicillin just didn't seem to work. But that's not all; it gets better. I was diagnosed with a brain tumour. Fortunately it was benign. But I had a surgery and received focused radiation. We've been through a lot. We are resting and taking it easy in these Covid times. I've declined online classes, and I'm catching up with my reading. How about you, bhai?'

Suryaveer discovered that the old desire to impress Aniruddha hadn't gone away in all the intervening years. 'I'm writing a book,' he said. 'It should be published next year.' The second statement was more a hope than a conviction. 'I was going through my bookshelf and found the old copy of *Lokayata* you had given me,' he continued. 'So I thought of you and decided to track you down.'

The Blind Matriarch

'Ah, good old Debiprasad!' Aniruddha said, in an expansive tone, his easy familiarity indicating that he had known the author personally. Which he hadn't. Then his tone became sharper, more focused. 'And how is the boy?' he asked. 'My nephew Samir? He would have turned eighteen in January, right?'

'Right,' Suryaveer replied. He had begun to sweat. He couldn't think of anything else to say. There was silence on both sides. Surya thought the line had dropped.

Then Aniruddha spoke again. 'I would like to talk to Samir, connect with him. Time is much too short, for all of us. It's time he got to know his real family, to accept them.'

'Yes. Those were my thoughts exactly,' Surya said tonelessly. 'I will speak to my son and discuss it with him. Perhaps we could set up a virtual meeting on Skype or Zoom to connect. Give me time, Aniruddha. I kept my promise to his mother. It's up to him to make his choices now.'

There was nothing more to say. Both of them had run out of words. Neither of them knew how to hang up. 'I will wait for your call, Surya,' Aniruddha said finally. 'And do message me your email. I will write to you tonight.'

Surya returned to his book. He went through his notes, collated his papers, but he couldn't concentrate. 'Dravidian primitive communism encounters Aryan patriarchal pastoralism,' he had scribbled on a lined yellow pad. This was followed by a diagrammatical example of agricultural–matriarchal practices and mother-rights countered by another chart of the pastoral-patriarchal traditions of male dominance. An arrow led to an underlined phrase 'Material Means of Subsistence' in double brackets.

Gobbledygook. What was his book even about? It was getting unwieldier by the day. He was no 'thought reformer' like D.P. Chattopadhyay. He was just an earnest seeker cataloguing his confusions and examining the contradictions around him.

A lapsed communist, a sceptical mystic, belonging neither to the right or the left, still searching for his centre.

Surya replaced the worn copy of *Lokayata*, with Aniruddha's inscription in black ink on the front page, to the top of the bookshelf from where he had extracted it. Samir had flagged a few pages with pink post-its before returning it to him. His son was grown-up now, and his heart and his head were big enough for him to learn to love his father's family without forgetting his adoptive one. Of that he was sure.

Upstairs, Matangi was lost in her daydreams. She was sifting through her memories, rearranging them by size and shape, by texture. There was the touch of a man's hand on her breast. The man was not her husband. He was thin and had thick curly hair. Only once, only that one time. He had smelt of soap and cigarette smoke. She had not been ashamed, of her body, of her acquiescence. She went back to this memory often, she savoured it in the remembrance, until the actual afternoon, that moment of lovemaking, had been revisited and replayed so many times that it had become another thing altogether.

What was his name? She had forgotten his name again; it rose and retreated in the tides of memory, of denial and recollection.

'Ravi,' she murmured. 'Ravi.'

Shanta was sitting by her bed. She heard her mother say the name out loud, then repeat it.

Matangi had fallen asleep again. 'Ravi,' she had said. 'Ravi.' There had been a note of longing in her voice. Shanta pondered the mystery, then decided to let it be. Some things were best left alone.

Her friend Babli Moitra had sent her a message. Shanta tried to call her back; the phone rang and rang until it disconnected. No reply. She realized she had been calling ACP Babli Mohan, not Babli Moitra as she had intended.

Her phone rang. It was Babli Mohan calling back. Only it wasn't. It was a male voice. 'Madam, you called my sister, Babli Mohan?' the man asked. 'Is it any important message, please? I am her brother speaking. Babli is in hospital, she has tested positive for Covid.'

'Is it serious?' she asked. 'Which hospital is she in?' She was inordinately shaken up. 'I am Shanta Sharma here. A friend of your sister's. I called by mistake but I'm around if you need me for anything.'

'I'm a medical intern at Loknayak Hospital,' he said calmly. 'My friends and colleagues are ensuring she gets the very best care. She will be well, Shanta-ji, with your good wishes.'

'I want to send food for her,' Shanta said wildly. 'And for you as well! Can I send some food to the hospital?'

'Not to the hospital,' he replied. 'But I will let you know when Babli comes back home, and you can call her then. I will send laddoos for you, sister. Worry not. We are good at clinical management at our government hospitals, and she is young and strong. Take care, sister, and I am here if you need me. Just call as you did just now, on Babli's number. Myself Suresh. Suresh Mohan. Namaste. Jai Hind.'

'Jai Hind.' She pondered the phrase long after Suresh Mohan had gone off the line. She loved her country with desperate passion, which was perhaps why she reacted so emotionally to its every misstep and aggravation.

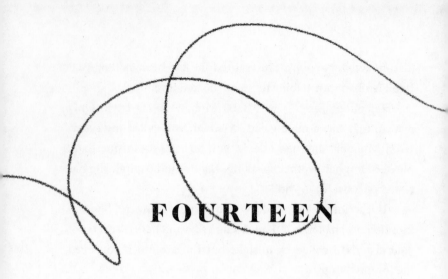

FOURTEEN

The call had been set up for the next day. Samir had coordinated the Zoom timings. He wondered if he should give himself a haircut. He wanted to look respectable for this first encounter.

He had come to terms with his two families—the one he had, the one he might have had. Nurture versus nature. He was secure here in C100, his love for his father Suryaveer unconditional, his devotion to his grandmother Matangi almost fanatical. But he wondered about his departed grandparents, his uncle, his still-to-be discovered cousins. He tried the other surname on his tongue, Samir Aditya Jha, then spat it out. That wasn't him, could never have been him.

It was in this state of mind that Samir discovered a news item on Twitter. He rarely read newspapers, and the increasingly leaner pages of the *Hindustan Times* and the *Indian Express* had very little to offer except statistics, placebos and pandemic panic.

A group of NASA scientists working on an experiment in Antarctica had unearthed data that seemed to point to a parallel universe. A cosmic ray detection experiment had discovered high-energy particles emanating from the earth, leading to speculation that the odd phenomenon indicated that the particles were actually travelling back in time.

He puzzled through the dense prose. 'The simplest explanation is that, at the moment of the Big Bang, 13.8 billion years ago, two universes were formed—ours and one that from our perspective is running in reverse with time going backward.'

That sounded cool. It was probably an elaborate hoax, but the thought stayed with him. The last three months had demonstrated that anything was possible. Anything at all. A virus had taken over the world. The magnetic poles were shifting. Asteroids steered away as they saw the mess that Planet Earth was in.

If time could travel backwards. If. Samir could return to his mother's womb, teach her not to be so rash. Maybe get her a job in an advertising agency in Mumbai. She could take him to visit his grandparents in Mangalore in the summer holidays. He could protect her from herself. If time could travel backwards. If.

His uncle sent a message asking if they could advance the Zoom call, as he had a doctor's appointment that had to be rescheduled. So there he was, sitting before the screen, waiting for the signal. And there was his uncle, an old man with a pleasant face. He wore what looked like diamond studs in his ears. His hair had been shaved off for the surgery, and there was thin stubble visible in places.

A face peered into the camera to say hello. Dark, shoulder-length hair, fine features, and a voice that sounded almost robotic. 'Hi, Samir! I am so delighted to meet a member of Aniruddha San's family. Namaste!' Hands joined in greeting. 'I do hope you are staying well.' No name. His uncle's partner seemed gender-nonconforming.

Aniruddha returned onscreen, flashing some photographs. 'Let me introduce you to your family. My mother, your grandmother. Your grandfather, my father. Digvijay Narain Jha and Tarakeshwari Jha.' A black-and-white photograph of two staring faces.

'Are they, my grandparents, still alive?' Samir asked tentatively.

His uncle shook his head sadly and wiped a tear from his eye. 'They passed away many years ago . . . 2008, to be precise. Within six months of each other.'

'And do you have any children, Uncle Aniruddha?'

'My partner, Yoshi Murasaki, whom you just met, is from Japan. We have been together for ten years now. We chose not to have children.'

'Ah, so,' Yoshi said, reappearing on the screen. 'You are our son now, Samir san!'

Samir wasn't sure how to respond. He silently thought of the abundance of parents that life seemed to be giving him. His uncle produced more photographs, colour pictures of an old house, a haveli, with hibiscus bushes and beds of roses laid out in the garden. Another photograph showed the same house, with mango trees laden with fruit, and litchis dangling from a bush in the foreground.

'This is your house, Samir,' his uncle said proudly. 'I have kept your father's portion, in your name, for when you can claim it. You will visit Bihar Sharif with Surya when you are ready.'

Surya had been lurking in the background all this while. 'Hello, Aniruddha,' he said. Then he fell silent. What was there to say, at this distance, after so much time?

'Hey, Surya, you have done a great job of bringing Samir up,' Aniruddha said to him. 'He is your son—he will always be your son—but we can claim him a bit too.'

Samir was suddenly desperate to end the conversation. 'Uncle Aniruddha, I have to go now,' he said smoothly. 'There are some online classes coming on, and I have to prepare for them. Let's talk again soon! I'm overwhelmed by this encounter. Namaste to Yoshi.'

He exited the Zoom call and burst into tears; he didn't know how to handle this. The drum set was not an answer any more. Smoking a joint wouldn't help either. Life was stranger than fiction. Of that he was sure.

Surya was relieved that Samir's first encounter with the Jha family was over. It was balm for his soul that he had not been overshadowed by his once-charismatic friend. Aniruddha Sharan Jha might possibly be an authority in his chosen field, but he appeared a much-diminished figure.

Surya decided to chat with Shanta about this milestone in his and Samir's life. She was the wisest, sanest, kindest person he knew, and her advice had stood him in good stead in every crisis.

But Shanta wasn't home. Now that the lockdown rules were somewhat relaxed, she had stepped out, driving to the Women for Peace office to catch up on things.

Munni was sitting on the sofa, stroking the cat, looking pensive. Surya sat down beside her.

'So, how are you doing, you and Shanta, under lockdown?' he asked. He was easy and comfortable with Munni, and she with him. She had nursed him through a debilitating attack of chikungunya fever, and their friendship had a firm foundation of mutual understanding. His question unleashed a torrent of anxieties.

'Shanta didi is very worried and upset ever since the policewoman Babliji got Covid. She feels she has just been sitting at home doing nothing to help people. So she has gone to her office today. But to tell you the truth, Surya saheb, I'm very worried too. This is my home, and Shanta didi and this cat are my family. But I have a son, and a daughter-in-law, and grandchildren. I worry about their safety. Day and night, day and night, I worry about their safety.'

Surya nodded his head sympathetically. What could he say? Everyone he knew was living in a state of suspended animation. He understood that she needed to tell somebody, and he was there to listen.

Something had triggered inside Munni. 'I want to tell you a story today, saheb—a story about a girl called Minu,' she said. 'That Minu, her father was a drunkard, and he had done bad things to his daughter. Then, one evening, that demon-father pushed her mother into the village well, the one near the peepal tree, and drowned her. The panchayat and the village elders ordered him thrown out of the village, not for killing his wife, but for polluting their well, which was for their upper-castes.'

'That girl Minu left the village as fast as she could. I was that Minu, until I ran away to Begusarai and changed my name to Munni. I worked as a maidservant, and then I got married.

'My husband was a drunkard too. He would beat me, every single day. Three times I dropped my children from my womb, because of his beatings.' She paused to wipe a tear from her eye with the corner of her dupatta, when Shanta rushed in, looking dishevelled and distressed.

'Thank God, you are here, Surya!' she exclaimed. 'We have to rush upstairs. Matangi-Ma seems to have taken ill. Lali just called.'

Matangi was lying in bed, head turned towards the wall. She had curled up like a little kitten, and was murmuring incoherently. She had kicked the Rajasthani quilt away and it lay on the floor. Shanta bent down to touch her mother's forehead. It was burning hot. She took her temperature—it stood at 102 degrees.

Lali picked up the quilt from the floor and began folding it. 'She has been like this since the bird left,' she said. 'Lying in bed, not eating properly.'

'You had better start wearing a mask when you are with Mataji, Lali,' Shanta said sternly. 'All of us must—all the time.'

Surya was already wearing a printed cotton mask from the stock that Anna Sen had gifted them. Lali got hers from the kitchen and positioned it over her nose and mouth.

'Pappoo too,' Shanta said.

'Pappoo has gone,' Lali replied. 'The sarkar has opened up movement now, so his other aunty, his father's cousin, came to take him back. They will go to Nepalgunj, by foot, by bus, whatever. He couldn't stay here forever, could he?'

Shanta stared at her in disbelief. 'You let that child go without telling us?' she exclaimed. Her voice was shaking with anger. 'It wasn't safe to let him go. We would have sent him—I would have sent him—when it was safe again, or at least safer.'

'Calm down, Shanta,' Surya said sternly. 'First things first. I've messaged Dr Nambiar. He is a gastroenterologist, but at least he is a doctor. He will be here soon. I'm going down to open the front door for him. You give her a cold compress. Wash your hands first. Wear gloves.'

Matangi had retreated deep into herself. She could hear voices, but they seemed to be coming from very far away. She was burning with fever. The heat inside her body was a stimulus, a reminder that she was still alive. She imagined rivers of fire flowing through her veins. Words and phrases tumbled out of nowhere and tangled inside her. Pappoo. Doctor. Gloves.

She thought she heard Shanta's voice and clutched at the sound. 'Mummy? Mummy? Don't worry, Mummy,' Shanta was saying. She could feel a cold towel on her face. A drop of mucus was stuck somewhere in her throat. She was choking and tried to spit it out.

Was this today or yesterday? Perhaps she was already dead. Were they preparing her for the funeral pyre, giving her a ritual bath? She would have to warn them that she was still alive.

The words stumbled out, as though they were falling from a precipice. 'I'm still alive,' she said. 'Still alive.'

'Of course, you are, Mummy,' Shanta replied affectionately. 'Nobody's going to let you die.'

Dr Nambiar had arrived. He was one of their neighbours. He stood at the door, masked and gloved. He slipped on surgical footpads over his shoes. 'How are you, Matangi-Ma?' he asked respectfully. Matangi, rumoured to be a hundred years old, was a legend in the neighbourhood.

Matangi had fallen back again, into that internal space she had been trying to scale. She heard him and tried to tell him she was fine, but the words would not emerge.

He took her temperature with a digital gun. Checked her oxygen levels and pulse rate with an oximeter. 'There are many types of fevers and infections going around,' he said. 'All of them cannot be attributed to the Covid virus. Let's observe her for two days, and then see what to do. Until then, paracetamol is the only answer. Two to three tablets a day. That's all. And keep her hydrated.'

But that was not all. 'No visitors to her room except caregivers. And they can't step out either. Strict quarantine rules apply. I wouldn't advise hospital. She might pick up the infection there even if she doesn't have it. No need to tell the neighbours. It would throw the Resident Welfare Association into an unnecessary panic. Let her heal. It might just be a flash fever.'

Shanta was shaken up. Surya was calm. Lali was flustered. Matangi seemed to be asleep; she was breathing slowly, normally.

'I had better tell Satish,' Surya said. 'He feels left out, sometimes, of these family decisions. And you pack up a small suitcase, Shanta, and move upstairs for a while, masks and all.'

Shanta lingered in the room, looking brokenheartedly at her mother. Should they seek further medical advice? Get her tested? Admit her to hospital? What was the best way to handle this?

Lali came and sat down beside her. She was smelling of sweat and garlic. Her approach to personal hygiene tended to be erratic, depending on her mood.

'I think you need to bathe, Lali,' Shanta said firmly. 'And to wear a mask indoors as well, as Mata-ji is unwell. But before that, we need to talk about Pappoo. It was wrong of you to let him go. You know it was. Can you track him, get him back?'

But she knew that wasn't possible any more, with Matangi so ill.

'Pappoo and his relatives are trying for a train. It's Ramzan, and they are still keeping their rozas, but they hope to be home before Eid. They will take another route to their house, so they can avoid the village quarantine. If they are lucky.'

Shanta could feel Pappoo's absence in the room. His curiosity, his quiet acceptance, his VROOM VRROOM. She started to weep, for Pappoo, for Babli Mohan, for Matangi.

Lali consoled her. 'Don't worry about Pappoo, Shanta didi. He was just a visitor here. We poor people are more hardy than you sahibs and memsahibs can ever understand. To tell you the truth, it's the bird I am missing. Mataji's rooh, her spirit, had got intertwined with that bird. These spirits exist, benign as well as malign, they really do.

My granduncle, my chachere dadaji, was a famous pir,' she continued. 'People would arrive from far and near for his magical remedies. He would prepare a naqsh and place it in a silver tabeez. His amulets could protect anybody from anything!'

Lali was usually tight-lipped about her family, about her Hindu and Muslim forbears, and let out information only in controlled and strategic outbursts. But she was in a different mood today.

'My granduncle could protect anybody from anything,' she continued. 'There would be a crowd of people outside his house on Tuesdays and Saturdays. He would tell them to buy a caged bird, from the local market—black hens or

141

a pair of mating doves—and set them free. It was one of his most efficacious remedies.' Then, suddenly, she began giggling. 'I will tell you a secret, Shanta didi, which only the members of our family knew. Those birds, which my pir uncle instructed believers to set free—we trained them to return to their owner. The doves would fly back home after they were set free. For the black hens, the believers would be told to set them free on a particular hilltop. The bird-keeper, my pir uncle's nephew, would collect them from the hilltop at night and sell them again.'

'It sounds like a good solution all around,' Shanta said thoughtfully. 'A win-win. Your pir uncle was a wise man; I can see that he was.'

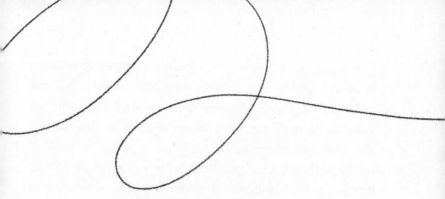

FIFTEEN

Surya saw the doctor off, then stopped at Satish's floor to tell him of Matangi's ill-health. 'Strict quarantine rules,' he explained. 'You cannot go and see her, though I suppose you could peep in through the door. And there's absolutely no need to let anybody know about this. We don't want her bundled off to a Covid hospital and the area to become a containment zone. Dr Nambiar says to wait two days before we take a call.'

Ritika took charge. 'You are right, Surya dada,' she said. 'Matangi-Ma needs to be isolated, and no one can care for her better than Shanta. We will just peep in for a moment, that's all, so that Satish and Rahul can say a silent prayer from the front door.'

Rahul looked grave. 'Matangi-Ma will be well soon,' he said. 'I can feel it in my bones. She has magical powers, and she is not ready to leave us just yet.'

They stood together at the door and peeped in. Not a word was said. Matangi lay curled up on the bed, covered with the Jaipuri quilt.

She stirred. 'Shanta,' she said, 'Shanta, the boy is at the door. My Rahul is standing there, waiting. I can see him. Give him the photographs—the pictures he wanted—from my steel cupboard.' Her voice was weak and slurred. She wasn't wearing her dentures, but her words, though garbled, were clear enough.

Nobody knew how to react. There were different registers of shock, surprise and relief on their faces. Only Rahul was unfazed. 'Thank you, Matangi-Ma,' he replied softly. 'We are going home now, Papa and Mama and me, so you can get some rest and recover quickly.'

Matangi had turned her head to the wall again. Satish and Ritika tiptoed out. Lali went to the veranda to make her evening phone calls. Shanta was alert to her mother's movements, but at another level she was lost in thought, trying to come to grips with the situation. Mataji was old but strong and alert. Her sixth sense had picked up Rahul's presence. She was hanging in there, for sure.

Matangi felt as though she were floating. Her arms hurt, her knees hurt, with an intensity of pain she had never felt before. She clicked with her tongue on the roof of her mouth, to centre herself, to make sense of what was going on inside her. It was a struggle. She could hear her father's voice. Her husband was sitting beside her on the bed, a gloomy expression on his face. 'Why are you taking so long?' he asked. Then she saw Rahul at the door, felt his love leap across to her. She had said something to him, she forgot what.

She tried to flag the pain, to keep track of it, to avert being drowned in it. She recognized the touch of Shanta's capable hands; she felt her spooning medicine into her mouth and tried not to choke on it. She was ready to depart, to leave her body, to drift away.

Shanta had been powdering the paracetamol and diluting it in water. It was a difficult task to spoon it into her mother's mouth. She did not resist, but it needed patience and coaxing. Matangi had lost control of her bladder and wetted the bed sheet. Lali and Shanta cleaned her up and changed the linen.

'Let her wear a kaftan,' Shanta said, 'and adult diapers.'

Surya was sent off to the chemist, and Shanta went to her cupboard to search the softest of her cotton kaftans. Matangi's cupboard was as ever meticulously organized in some mysterious inner order. Shanta's eyes skimmed through the contents. Her underwear, her saris, blouses and petticoats. Four kaftans. The hand-embroidered handkerchiefs folded neatly in a corner of the shelf. A rag doll her mother had stitched for her when she was a little girl. Medicines. Mysterious pouches of various sizes. A packet of biscuits. On the bottom shelf of the steel cupboard, some folders.

She looked through the folders, more from a sense of duty than curiosity. The first folder was titled 'LAST WILL AND TESTAMENT'. Shanta was surprised, shocked, angry. How could her mother have kept her in the dark or made a will without consulting her? Which of her sons could have put her up to it? Surely not Suryaveer? Satish?

The folder was empty. It contained nothing, just the tantalizing title, which had been printed and pasted on the plastic folder. There was another larger file next to it, a blue plastic box-file, hidden under a pile of bedsheets. It contained a bunch of photographs, of different sizes and varying vintage.

Shanta was still seething with indignation at the discovery of 'the last will and testament', although she realized this was not the moment to react to it. She took a deep breath and calmed herself down. There had to be a logical explanation. She knew her mother, trusted her mother. She took out the photographs and placed them on the table by the window. She would search through them later for the pictures Rahul needed for his 'family tree' project.

The constant doses of paracetamol had brought Matangi's temperature down. It hovered around a hundred, and she seemed more comfortable. Dr Nambiar called. 'It may be Covid, but then it may not. All I can say is that as per your reports she seems to be recovering. Let me know of any further developments.'

Shanta was washing her hands compulsively, sanitizing every surface in the room. She would wear two masks, one over the other. It was getting to her—Matangi's silent battle, Lali's whispered phone conversations, the spiralling disasters on television and social media. Forty trains transporting migrants to their home states had taken off to mistaken destinations and lost their way. Swarms of locusts had attacked Rajasthan, and now Madhya Pradesh. China and Nepal were escalating a military confrontation.

These were not just bad times. This was apocalypse. Kalyug.

She missed her flat, the comfort of her room. She missed Trump. She missed Munni. She found Lali's continued company intolerable. It was a nightmare. Shanta had always considered herself a natural caregiver. She was patient, and kind, and not easily perturbed. But self-isolating with her mother was not bringing out the best in her. She felt claustrophobic and ill-tempered and snappy.

She decided to divert herself by sorting out the photographs in Matangi's cupboard and locating some for Rahul. She found one of her father, Prabodh Kumar Sharma, and one of Matangi's father and her grandfather, Matang Singh Kashyap. There was a photograph of her parents together, their calm smiles belying the stress and tension that had existed between them all through their marital lives.

There was another old photograph, one that took her completely by surprise. It was a face she recognized, a face she had seen before, in another old photograph. A foreigner, a white woman, wearing a dress, standing near a beach. She had a casual hairstyle and a carefully held smile.

She turned the photo over. A conscientious handwriting, a message written in cobalt blue ink. 'From Galina, with love. Yalta 1985'.

Galina. Her father's girlfriend. Shanta had found a photograph in his papers, when she was sorting things out after his death. Like most defence ministry officials of his day and age, he had made regular official visits to the Soviet Union. Honey traps were par for the course in military purchases, but the girl in the photograph didn't fit the stereotype of a seductress. There was an innocence to the photograph, an innocence that felt odd when it adhered to her father. Perhaps Galina had loved her father, perhaps her father had loved Galina. Perhaps they had just been friends. It was all a story now, a long-ago love story.

There had been the scandal later, and the enquiry. Her father had insisted that he was just a scapegoat, that he had nothing to do with the misdirected Vostro funds, that there were important politicians involved. Shanta had overheard tense conversations, when she was young, and pieced them together, as children do.

How much had her mother known, she wondered. How had the photograph reached her? Had she ever seen it, what with her rapidly failing eyesight?

Once, when she was young, Shanta had asked Matangi a question about her father. Her mother didn't usually resort to English words, but she did then. 'Your father is a womanizer,' her mother had said. 'And I am increasingly blind to it.'

The memory of Matangi-Ma's words, of the look in her eyes, reverberated through the tiny dressing room. How her beloved mother had suffered at the hands of that monster. In darkness when she closed her eyes and in darkness when she opened them. What must that feel like? Impulsively, she shut the door and switched off the lights. Blinded by a slow trickle of tears, she felt her way along the walls of the room. She felt the terrycloth towel hanging on a hook, the chipped wooden table with its bottles of hair oils and cold cream, the cool metal of the medicine cabinet beside it. This room that her mother sensed and knew so well. The darkness had closed in on her; she could feel the weight and texture of it change. Was it only the absence of light? She stood there for a long time, lost in the shadows. Then she opened her eyes, switched on the light and opened the door.

Her mother was stronger than the darkness, she was the essence of light. And the past, it was in the past. She took the photographs of her parents and the portrait of her grandfather, of Matangi's father, to be kept aside for Rahul's project. She put the rest of them back, in the steel cupboard, under the linen.

Matangi was stirring. She wanted tea, she said. Lali bustled off to make some. Shanta went to the veranda, for a breather. It was scorching hot outside. The temperature had shot up to the high forties. Forty-four degrees. Forty-five degrees. She breathed the heat in, defying it, challenging it.

A strange sight met her eyes. There were five crows lined up on the balcony wall. They weren't doing anything, just sitting there, and they didn't fly away when they saw her. Instinctively, she went to the kitchen and put out a plastic bowl of water in a corner of the balcony for them.

Matangi sat up and cooled the tea with her breath before she sipped it. She felt empty, drained, swept clean. It was as though there was just a shell, of what had once been her—a husk, a hollow, untenanted room.

Lali was watching her intently. 'You will be well again soon, Mataji,' she said 'You are stronger than all the others who live here in C100, stronger than all of them put together. You will be well.'

Matangi didn't register her words. She couldn't register anything. The pain moved around her frail frame like an avalanche. She had become the pain. Her still-nimble senses were registering its journey across the battlefield of her body, buffering it as best as they could.

Ritika was sitting in the lotus posture on her yoga mat, trying to centre herself. Matangi's illness had shaken her up more than she had ever thought possible. The unspoken fears, the anxieties that she had been carrying around through the last few months converged in that one overriding fear.

For a single child in a nuclear household, marrying into a joint family had been like getting a visa to live in a foreign country. It meant encountering a new language, with inflections she could never learn, and unwritten laws, unspoken caveats. It didn't help that Satish was the pampered youngest sibling, and that it had been an arranged marriage. She had felt constantly on trial, assessed by their scrutiny, and her outward calm had been maintained at a great cost to herself.

Ritika had always been afraid of loss. Where had that sense of deprivation, of forfeiture, come from, she wondered. What childish tragedy had triggered it? Was it the pocket money taken back because she lost her geometry box? The wristwatch her parents had bought, but never given her, because . . . she had forgotten the reasons, the sequence, but she remembered how she had felt when what should have been hers was so often unfairly withheld.

She tried some stretches. The strange times the world was passing through had both intensified and soothed Ritika's anxieties. Her panic when Compass International seemed on the brink of collapse had been countered by Girish Syal's almost miraculous pull back.

'We are all in this together, Ritika,' he had told her. And indeed, everybody did seem to be in this together, in crisis, in tragedy, in the unexpected implosion of the model of the world they had known and believed in.

The first thing she had done when she received some much-delayed dues from Compass was to dig into her savings and pay up for a year in advance for her mother's care. She had earlier always paid on a monthly basis, convincing herself that this was the more practical thing to do. If her mother were to pass away, to suddenly drop dead, it would be difficult and also ungracious to push for a refund. 'Better to pay month by month, and take it as it comes,' she had told herself. It was an enormous mental relief to have paid up for a year. Her duties were now confined to weekly phone calls, as travel seemed an almost impossible option in the year ahead. Unless.

A long patch of deep breathing. But her mind kept wandering. Everything stood at 'unless'. Her phone rang. It was her hairdresser—her child was sick, and she couldn't get medical help.

Ritika, normally not one to tangle with other people's problems, called an ex-colleague whose wife was a doctor and managed an OPD appointment with a paediatrician at the hospital where she worked.

'We are all in this together,' she told the hairdresser when she tried to thank her.

The Sens were celebrating their wedding anniversary with a private date in the garden. The temperature was stuck in the forties, even after sunset, but they were not deterred. Anna had cooked spicy roast chicken with buttered noodles, and a Bengali style chochori. There was a cherry tart for dessert—actually two cherry tarts, with one kept aside for Shanta and her family.

They were seated on the dusty cane chairs she had dragged out from the front porch. Anna's heart was set on a candlelight dinner, so she brought out a torch and upended it to simulate a flame. There was a buzz of mosquitoes around them. She squished a shower of herbal insect repellent on his face, his arms. Her husband regarded her fondly from across the table. Anna was the best thing that had ever happened to him, though she could be alarmingly unpredictable.

A love story remembered. It was early in his career, when he was still a junior diplomat. He had been assigned a translator, Anna Kowalski. She knew Polish, a little Hindi and a little English. He knew only English, Sanskrit, Bangla, a little Hindi and few words of Polish. She was astoundingly pretty. They fell in love and got married.

Anna had followed him around the world as a foreign service wife, making samosas and pierogi, valiantly pinning up her silk saris, and mostly remaining unflustered by his occasional flashes of bad temper.

Agastya Sen had always been dubbed 'odd' by his colleagues. He read Sanskrit as a hobby. He spoke very little. The bouts of temper were legend. He mellowed after marriage, as Anna had a knack for handling him. They agreed on everything except pets. Mr Sen hated dogs and was allergic to cat's hair. Anna had always kept cats, before marriage, and longed for a kitten. Still, a no-pet household was a small price to pay for marital harmony.

'So, we turn eighty-four,' Mr Sen said reflectively, holding up a glass of Chenin Blanc to his wife. She was drinking beer and raised her glass of Kingfisher in cheery response.

Agastya Sen was born in Patna when King George V was still King Emperor. He would turn eighty-four on 24 June. His father had died in the Quetta earthquake of May 1935, just weeks before he came into the world. His mother had returned to her parents in Asansol after that and sacrificed everything for his education. Ma had been alive to share in the splendour of the Warsaw residence in his last ambassadorial posting, and for that he was grateful.

Anna Kowalski was born in Krakow in July 1935. The chief of state Józef Pilsudski had just died, leaving the country a dictatorship without a dictator. She had grown up in German-occupied Poland, and under communist rule under the Soviets after that.

They raised their glasses again. 'We have been through a lot, darling,' he said. 'Kidnappings and gangsters and everyday trials, and we have weathered the storms.'

Anna was blushing. Mr Sen had called her 'darling' only once before, when he had proposed to her. 'We have survived,' she affirmed, 'and we will survive—Covid, old age and all that—and live to be a hundred. At least.'

SIXTEEN

The NASA news item about parallel worlds had left Samir intrigued. He looked up more on the subject on the net. 'The Many World Interpretation (MWI) of quantum mechanics holds that there are many worlds that exist in parallel at the same space and time as our own.'

That sounded extremely reasonable.

'In particular, every time a quantum experiment with different possible outcomes is performed, all outcomes are obtained, each in a different world, even if we are only aware of the world with the outcome we have seen.'

That made sense too.

'Yay!' he told himself. 'Samir Sharma can understand quantum physics!'

Life was like a Terry Pritchett novel, he decided, like poker in a pitch-dark room. Anything could happen, anytime, anywhere. The last few weeks had made him realize all the possible lives he might have lived. Perhaps there were other options playing out even now in a parallel universe. It felt like an interactive novel, with open-ended endings—and beginnings.

His uncle, Aniruddha Sharan Jha, had been bombarding Samir with emails and text messages. It was all getting a bit tiring really, although Samir was touched by the tenacity with which his newfound chacha was staking his blood claim.

'Dearest Samir' the emails would begin, and sign off with 'Ever Yours, Uncle Aniruddha'.

Each mail would have multiple attachments, scanned photographs and links. Samir didn't bother to read or reply to them, though he responded to the emojis with further affectionate emojis and smiley faces.

Rahul came down to their floor to work on the family tree. His father came down with him as well. Samir was surprised to see him, as Uncle Satish was shy, even reticent, in his interactions with the rest of the family. The shops had begun to open up as the lockdown slowly eased out, and Satish had accompanied his son to the stationers to stock up on glue sticks, blue tack, masking tape, coloured markers, and sheets of stiff white cardboard.

They unloaded the stack of stationery on the dining table. Rahul brought out the sheaf of photographs he had got together, but they were all of different sizes and shapes, and the whole exercise seemed somehow unwieldy.

Satish came up with an idea. 'Let's do it virtually,' he said. 'I will help you. We could even structure it as a PowerPoint presentation.'

They spread the photos out on the cardboard sheet first, in a rough timeline. They began with Matangi's father, Matang Singh Kashyap. Born 1905, died 15 August 1950.

'My grandfather was born in 1908,' Satish volunteered.

'How did you know that, Papa?' Rahul asked, bestowing an admiring look on his father.

'I know more than I let on,' Satish said. 'I have all sorts of facts and figures stored up in my skull.'

Matangi came next. They chose an old photograph of her, where she was seated regally on a carved chair, wearing dangling earrings. Prabodh Kumar Sharma appeared too, looking stern and disapproving. The photographs of Ritika's parents, Sriram and Kaveri Tiwari, were placed below, with blue and black wavy lines, and secured with blue tack.

The next chart was laid out with photos of Surya, Shanta, Satish and Ritika. 'Hold on,' Samir said and brought back the photograph of his mother, Samira, from his room. 'My uncle Aniruddha has sent one of my father Aditya Sharan Jha. I will download and print that.'

'My father. Aditya Sharan Jha.' Samir tasted the words on his lips, and he smiled.

The boys, Samir and Rahul, came next. Rahul had chosen a picture where he was in school uniform, receiving a scholar badge. Samir had found one where he was on a trek, a steep hill looming over him.

Munni walked in just then, with a casserole full of fragrant biryani. She was bored with nothing to do, she said, and decided to cook for Surya. Rahul took a photo of her as well for the project. Lali was quarantined with Matangi-Ma, but Samir would find one of her.

'And Pappoo!' Rahul said. 'We must have Pappoo in the family tree as well.'

'I will get a photo from Lali once Matangi-Ma is better,' Samir said. They fell silent for a moment. They had all been avoiding mentioning Matangi's illness even though it was uppermost in their minds.

'Let's take these to my study,' Satish said. 'We will scan the pictures, fill in the missing dates and tabulate it all. I will take three printouts on glossy paper, for Rahul, Samir and myself. We are family, and we are all in it together.'

But first they had the biryani. Surya and Satish, Samir and Rahul. They ate in Surya's study, piled high with flyaway papers and notes for his book, as the dining table was much too messy, what with all the bits of paper and glue and scattered photographs. After that, they trooped up to the floor above, and Surya returned to his notes.

He was still struggling with the theme that would hold his ambitious writing project together, and began searching the heap of books on the floor until he found A.K. Ramanujan. Surya turned to the page he had flagged, and softly read out the lines to himself, with all the varied inflections.

Is there an Indian way of thinking?
Is there *an* Indian way of thinking?
Is there an *Indian* way of thinking?
Is there an Indian way of *thinking?*

The book had his notes pencilled on the margins. ' . . . refers to A.K.R. as a "progressive fence sitter"'. He was still toying with the phrase when Munni walked in.

'There's something I want to tell you, Surya dada,' she said, 'something I have never told anyone before.'

Surya was mildly annoyed by her intrusion but tried not to show it. He put aside his notes and gestured to her to sit down.

'There was something I began telling you, that day when we were talking, and then Mataji fell ill. Shanta didi is upstairs with her, and I am all alone at home, with nothing to do. The past keeps coming back to me, Surya dada, like a flashback from a flim.'

She had called a film a 'flim', as she always did. His mind was still on Ramanujan. What was she going on about?

'I have committed a crime,' she said. 'The greatest crime any human being can commit. That night, when my father killed my mother, and the villagers chased him away, he came to see me. I didn't let him into our house, if you could call that hovel a house.' She wiped a tear from her eye. 'I told him I would meet him by the well, the same well where my mother had drowned. He was drunk, he was afraid. He said he would give himself up to the police, if I wanted. I said I didn't want to get involved with the police, nobody in the village wanted to get involved with the police, which was why the villagers had chased him away.'

Surya was listening. He could picture the scene she was so vividly describing.

'So my father leaned over the well and began wailing for my mother, imploring her to come back. I told him Mother was dead but he kept calling to her. So, I . . .' Her voice quavered here. 'So I pushed him over, into the well. "You can meet Mother now!" I screamed down the well, and then I ran, and ran, and ran. I took a bus, I took a train, I found myself in Begusarai.'

Surya was horrified by her story, but not surprised. He had lived in the badlands of Bihar, encountered such tales of brutality before. He didn't know how to respond, how to comfort her. 'Begusarai,' he said reflectively. 'I've been to Begusarai.'

'My mother's spirit looked after me, from heaven. I got a job, I cleaned and swabbed, and later I learnt to cook as well. I was honest and hardworking. My employers were good to me. But the memory of what I had done tormented me.'

Surya leaned over and held her hand.

'I couldn't sleep. I would weep through the night. His ghost would come to me at night, soaking wet. I went to see a Babaji in the temple. He told me to go to the riverfront, to the Ganga, and bathe there once a week. Any day of the week that I could. I did it all those years I lived in Begusarai. Even now, I keep Gangajal with me, and I sprinkle it over myself once a week.'

'You were a child then,' Surya said soothingly. 'You wait here and I will get you some tea.'

'I don't want any tea,' Munni said. 'And you know what? I may have been a child then, but I would do it again, I would push him down the well again, if I had to. I was afraid to tell anyone, all these years. Afraid of the police. Afraid of my employers. Afraid of my husband. Afraid of my son. But now I have told you my secret.'

She bent down to touch his feet. He stepped back, embarrassed, and wiped the tears from her eyes. Then she left the room. What could he say? What could he do to share her hurt?

He had spent a fortnight in Begusarai. It had been the hotspot of activism in those days. 'The Leningrad of India'—that's what they used to call it. There was another recollection attached to Begusarai. The 'people's poet' Ramdhari Singh Dinkar, the author of *Rashmirathi*, had been born in district Begusarai. Munni's story had moved him deeply, brought alive the mixed memories of that land of poetry and pain. '*Koi Mujhe Bata De, Kya Aaj Ho Raha Hai.*'

He tried to return to his notes. 'Behind the apparent diversity, there is a unity in Indian thought, characterized by contradiction, inconsistency and context-sensitivity.' But his mind was not on Ramanujan any more. He sat down cross-legged on the floor, facing the south, and recited the Mahamrityunjaya mantra three times. It was a prayer for the living and the dead. It was a prayer for Matangi-Ma as well as Munni, and for her dead father too. Then he put away his notes and went for a walk in the park.

Matangi felt as though she had been left adrift between clumps and clusters of pain. She attempted to take stock of what was going on inside her. First she tried to twitch her toes. They were leaden and unresponsive. Her calves and knees were hurting, as were her wrists and elbows. Her chest felt congested, as did her nasal passages. It was difficult to breathe from her nose or her mouth, and yet she was not choking. She tried to click her tongue against the roof of her mouth, but she couldn't manage it. It was as though there was an insurrection going on inside her body; it had become a battleground with no interludes of peace.

The Blind Matriarch

And then a river of words entered into the nightmare, streams and strings of words, without pattern or meaning, English words she did not understand and Hindi words she had never learnt. Swear words, foul and filthy words, like those her husband had sometimes used.

Lali was watching Matangi toss and turn. She was muttering incoherently, English and Hindi and some swear words that made Lali blush. Ah well, she told herself, master, mistress, servant, we were all humans in the end, and death and this virus disease didn't discriminate between rich and poor, Hindu or Muslim. Though the poor had the worst of it, always.

Pappoo had sent her a WhatsApp photo. He was at a railway station, wearing a red tee shirt and a jauntily reversed baseball cap. He looked happy.

What would happen to Lali if, when, Mataji died? She had become fond of the old woman, but she was reconciled to her departure, now or whenever. Suryaveer would employ her, but there was no work to be done there; it was a bachelor household and would become even more so after Samir returned to college.

And Ritika. Lali couldn't imagine working with Ritika. She was of that other breed of employers—Lali had seen many of them—who drew a line, a Lakshman Rekha, between servants and masters. She did try to be kind, Lali wouldn't deny that, but . . .

And what would happen to this flat on the top floor, she wondered. They wouldn't rent it out, they surely wouldn't. 'I will leave a gift for you, some money, after I am gone,' Mataji had told her once. Perhaps that had only been a passing fancy. Matangi was old, but not forgetful. It was too late to remind her now.

Matangi was moaning again. Lali smoothed her forehead and began gently massaging her withered hands.

Shanta sat down on the floor beside Lali. She was dutifully taking Matangi's temperature, spooning her paracetamol, doing all the things she had to. She felt hollow inside, completely devastated. She couldn't imagine life without her mother.

But her mother seemed to be weathering the storm. Her temperature varied between 100 and 102 Fahrenheit, and she was taking in tiny morsels of food. Shanta had called Dr Nambiar, and their family GP, Dr Sangita Gupta. She wanted Matangi-Ma in the hospital, in the ICU, but Surya calmed her down.

'The hospitals are hotbeds of infection,' he cautioned. 'That's what Dr Nambiar implied, in so many words. Let's give it another day or two, Shanta. Home is the safest place for her to recover.'

Surya had made a bargain with the gods. He had resolved to become a teetotaller and a strict vegetarian. The chicken biryani Munni had brought up had posed a dilemma, as he didn't want to discuss his newfound vegetarianism. He had spooned a small portion onto his plate and wandered over to the kitchen, where he threw it into the garbage bin.

His instincts told him his mother would recover, that her body, which had weathered so many challenges, would negotiate its way out of illness. But the vegetarianism was non-negotiable, as was the abstinence from alcohol. These were vows he would keep all his life.

Munni walked in again, with yet another tray in her hands, containing a half portion of luscious-looking cherry tart. Anna Sen had left it for Shanta and the family, she informed him, and she had already taken the other half up for Rahul and his parents. Her manner and demeanour were back to normal, and neither made mention of what had passed between them.

Surya had not eaten the fragrant biryani, and he was beginning to feel hungry. He wolfed down a generous portion of the tart, thanking the stars that Anna had sent such a delicious vegetarian offering.

Samir joined him and demolished the rest. 'I've been thinking,' he said, wiping the remnants of the cherry tart from his face, 'I've been thinking about life.'

Surya raised an eyebrow. 'That's a good beginning,' he said, 'but a rather vast subject to contemplate.'

'I think all of us think that everybody's lives follow a common reality, but they don't! There are people whose lives were destined to be different from the day they were born. Their fates are made from a different fabric, cut to a different pattern. More things happen to them—joyful things, hurtful things. And there are others whose lives run smoothly, forever, so smoothly that you would imagine them dying of boredom. I've been wondering, which of them is the luckier, or the unluckier?'

Surya smiled, but a worried question lurked behind his eyes. 'That's an interesting hypothesis, son,' he said. 'Do let me know when you reach any further conclusions.'

Upstairs, on the top floor, Shanta was standing in the veranda, sipping a mug of strong masala chai. The crows had arrived again. There were five of them sitting peaceably on the balcony wall, staring at her with their clever, curious eyes. They began an orchestrated conversation of harsh caws. She felt they were including her in their talk. She brought some bread from the kitchen but they disdained it. Two of the crows hopped about before flying away. The others remained steadfast at their posts.

Shanta poured some water into the plastic bowl she had set out for them and returned to her mother's room feeling more at peace with herself.

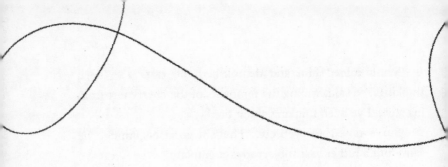

SEVENTEEN

Rahul was quizzing his father with some riddles.

'It belongs to you, but your friends use it more. What is it?' he asked.

Satish looked puzzled. 'Let me think . . .' he said. Then: 'I give up.'

'It's your name!' Rahul announced excitedly. 'Your name belongs to you, but your friends use it more. Get it?'

'Got it!' Satish responded.

'If you don't keep me, I will break. What am I?'

Satish hadn't stopped worrying about his mother. Shanta had set up a strict isolation region. Samir had established a family WhatsApp group which Shanta updated several times a day, where they kept track of Matangi's health. He was trying to keep Rahul occupied, although he suspected that it was possibly the other way around.

'If you don't keep me, I will break. What could that be?' Satish mused aloud.

'A promise!' Rahul declared excitedly. 'That's why you should always keep your promises, Papa! Just one more,' Rahul continued. 'There's only one word in the dictionary that's spelt wrong. What is it?'

Satish smiled broadly. He knew this one. 'It's the word wrong!' he replied. 'W-R-O-N-G! That's the right spelling, though. I have to make some calls now, so no more riddles for now. But thank you for amusing—and educating—me.'

Rahul's expression turned serious. 'There's something I want to tell you, Papa,' he said. 'Something I've learnt from all of us being together in lockdown. It's serious—a grown-up thing.'

He handed Satish a large white envelope. 'It's for you, Papa, and you can share it with Mummy too,' he said earnestly. The envelope had a handwritten note penned carefully on stiff cardboard, which had been cut around the edges in a zigzag design. This is what it said: 'WHAT I HAVE LEARNT: That Your Generation May Have Forgotten, or not known. There are things in life you can't prepare for. In the end, we have to learn as we grow.'

Had he found this on the internet? Whatever the source, their son was wiser than Ritika and him put together. Satish gave him a solemn kiss on his forehead. 'I'll share this with Mummy,' he promised. 'Thank you for reminding us of such an important lesson.'

Matangi was still fighting the pain. She had mapped its movements by now, and it was almost a game to track it. She felt detached, in free fall, until suddenly, she spiralled into a still centre of silence within herself. She stumbled upon it almost by accident—a place where she felt nothing, where all was still and awaiting.

She could hear the crows cawing. She thought she saw a light, and then it was the orb of the moon.

'So, it's a full moon tonight,' she said to herself wonderingly. She felt calm and at peace in the darkness, which the moon could not banish, and the silence, with only the crows cawing somewhere in the distance.

Shanta heard her, and her eyes filled up with tears. Her mother seemed lost in a labyrinth. 'The sun is still shining outside, Mummy,' she said, tenderly smoothing Matangi's hair. But the old woman heard nothing, registered nothing.

Shanta was working herself into a frenzy. Her mother was ill. It was clear she needed to be in a hospital or under medical supervision. She would never forgive herself if anything went wrong. She called up their GP, who had advised them after Dr Nambiar's visit.

Dr Sangita was her usual calm and soothing self, but her voice indicated that she was cracking under the pressure. 'I feel so helpless,' she confessed. 'Hospitals are potential hotspots. In these surreal times you should just stay put at home and wait and watch. And pray. She might surprise you!'

So that was that. Shanta was too empty and exhausted to pray. She went out to the veranda again, for a breather. She had quit smoking a long time ago, but she would have given anything for a cigarette just then. Or a drink.

She glared at the crows. Why had they taken up summer residence in Matangi-Ma's veranda? She stamped her feet and waved her hands to shoo them away, but they paid no heed. And then, suddenly, they rose as one and flapped threateningly over her head. 'You are the intruder here,' they seemed to say. Then they flew off, in different directions.

'A murder of crows,' Sharda told herself wryly. Really, Matangi-Ma drew the strangest presences.

Just then, Lali came rushing out. 'Mataji is up!' she said. 'She is well again. Mashallah!'

Shanta stumbled back into the room. She was wonderstruck to see Matangi sitting up. Her crumpled cream kaftan had ridden up to her knees. She looked confused, but in control of herself.

'I want some tea,' she said in a perfectly normal voice.

Her mother was indestructible, shatterproof. She could negotiate anything.

After she had sipped at the tea and had half a biscuit, she fell back on the bed again, but with her head flat on the pillow, not turned to the wall as it often was.

Shanta checked her temperature. It was normal, at 98 Fahrenheit. She seemed to have little recollection of being so very ill. 'I'm feeling a bit better now,' she declared, and went back to sleep.

Shanta rushed to inform the family WhatsApp group. 'Let's wait and watch,' Surya advised. There was very little else to do, really.

Shanta received a message from Babli Mohan. 'Thank you for checking on my health. Now recovering. Sincerely, Babli Mohan.'

That was the evening there was a sudden thunderstorm, and a double rainbow was sighted over the city. The summer squall had passed. Shanta felt a shift of mood, a lightening of apprehension. Perhaps her mother was feeling better. Perhaps the planet was healing. Perhaps.

Matangi was asleep and breathing normally. Lali was in the veranda, whispering into her phone. The lockdown was due to lift the next day, on the first of June. Life would swing back to normal, like an elastic band held too long. There was a feeling of '*dekhi jayegi*' all around. The doctors were warning of an expected spike in infections, and the death count was going up every day, but most people's patience had run out.

She rung up Babli Mohan. The policewoman picked up the phone. She sounded dispirited and tired. 'I am recovering slowly, Shantaji,' she said. 'I'm full of aches and pains, and my appetite has completely gone. I can't smell the food, I can't taste it. My brother has insisted that I stay at home, but for somebody like me that's the most difficult thing to do.'

'What's your favourite dish?' Shanta asked her. 'Shut your eyes and imagine what you might be tempted to eat.'

Babli's voice cheered up discernibly at the other end. 'I would like some kadhi-chawal. Or maybe some rajma-chawal.'

Shanta found herself smiling too. 'Send me your address, Babli,' she said. 'I will send you a special treat tomorrow, to mark the city opening out! Life has to go on . . .'

Babli protested, told Shanta not to take the trouble. 'Don't worry, Babli, this gives me more joy than it does you!' she replied.

'You are a real Ma Annapurna,' Babli said emotionally. 'And how are your mad neighbours? I've forgotten their names. I hope they are not giving you too much trouble?'

'The Sens are fine,' Shanta replied, but the phone had disconnected.

Ma Annapurna, Babli had called her. The goddess of food and plenty. It was true that she did not know how to express her affection in any way other than by offerings of food. It gave her joy to cook, to watch people eat. The lockdown and the meals cooked for the Women and Peace collective, had taken that to another level.

But there was surely something wrong, something reductive, even pathetic, to bring every human emotion to the exchange of foodstuffs. What had happened to all the friends who had been such an intrinsic part of her life? Where had they vanished?

Shanta took a deep, hard dive within herself. She had excellent relationships with professional colleagues around the world. She was always there for anyone in trouble. She appeared almost saintly in the mirror of self-scrutiny. But was she doing the best she could for herself? Where were the small joys, the intimacies, the laughter? When was the last time she had enjoyed a good gossip? What was wrong with her?

She sat down wearily and confronted the truth. She was lonely. That, in six letters, was the sum and story of her situation. L-O-N-E-L-Y. Isolated. Alone. Friendless. Forsaken.

It had not always been so. She had retreated into herself, step by step. It was comforting to be alone. She enjoyed her own company, but perhaps she had wandered too deep into herself, without even noticing.

She would reorient herself, she promised. She would reach out again, she would laugh and gossip and re-socialize. She would host a dinner party for her friends when the pandemic eased out—a socially distanced dinner party but one that would bring friends together under her roof.

Matangi had woken up. 'I don't want to wear this kaftan,' she declared, her voice weak but firm. 'Get me some normal clothes, please.'

Lali and Shanta exchanged smiles. 'Yes, Mataji,' Lali said, 'and what do you want to eat?'

'I want mangoes!' she said, a note of longing in her voice. 'And some curd.' She seemed well, and mysteriously unaware of the ordeal she had been through.

Shanta sent a photo of Matangi sitting up to Dr Sangita, who replied with a thumbs-up emoji. 'Keep her rested, and hydrated, and isolated. Keep her cheerful. It sounds as though it was a flash fever. I will check her parameters tomorrow morning on the phone.'

She forwarded the picture and the doctor's message to the family, then decided to go down to her flat for a while. She needed to shower and shampoo in the comfort of her own bathroom, then to stretch out and have a drink.

Shanta had a long warm shower and a luxurious shampoo. She emerged from the bath with a towel wrapped round her head, planning to settle down with a single malt whiskey, or a Jack Daniels with just the two cubes of ice. She would catch up with television news; she had been out of touch with the world for a while.

But the cat had vomited in a corner of the living room. Munni helped Shanta clean the mess up. Poor Miss Trump must have missed her, and picked up the stress overload. After the floor was cleaned and a Neroli incense stick lit up to clear the smell, she settled on the sofa with Miss Trump and stroked her orange fur. Something was different about the contours of her stomach—it seemed swollen and distended. She looked up at Shanta and purred, as though telling her something. There was a movement in her belly, something was stirring inside.

Shanta held her paw and looked into her amber cat-eyes. 'I know the signs,' she said. 'You are pregnant, aren't you? I'm sorry I didn't notice all these days. It'll be all right. Munni and I are there for you.'

She called Munni out from the kitchen. 'We are going to become grandparents!' she said excitedly. 'Miss Trump is due any day now! Yay!'

'Good news!' Munni responded, and brought Shanta a laddoo from the batch she had cooked for time-pass while there was nothing to do.

So, they sat and watched television together, Shanta and Trump, to see what devastation her cat's namesake was wreaking upon the world. The Houston police chief was on air, speaking to Christiane Amanpour. 'Let me say just this to the President of the United States, on behalf of the police chiefs of the country: please, if you don't have something constructive to say, keep your mouth shut.'

Munni had soaked the rajma and set the curd for the meal that had to be sent to the policewoman. It was good to have Shanta back at home.

It was late into the night. Rahul and Samir were sitting in Samir's room. They had put the lights out and lit just two fragrant vanilla-scented candles. There were shadows all around them. They were listening to Frank Sinatra.

'*I did it my way.*'

The lockdown was gradually being lifted, but they were all being careful in C100 because of Matangi's health. Samir was planning to leave the next morning to stay for a few days with a friend at his farmhouse. The last three months had brought them both closer than ever, and Rahul and Samir had decided to hang out together in the evening. Dollar was ensconced comfortably between them, listening in occasionally with one raised ear.

'I want to learn to play the drums, Samir dada,' Rahul confided.

'Anytime, yaar, walk into my room, settle on the hot seat, and start practising! You could scroll through the online coaching sessions and see which ones work for you,' Samir said. 'You could even take the drums to your room. That might make it even easier.'

Rahul shuddered. 'Ma—she will go absolutely crazy,' he said. 'Surya chacha is ever so much more patient.'

A lizard darted across the shadows on the wall. Samir saw it and began screaming, clutching at Rahul for comfort. He was phobic about creepy-crawlies, about lizards and spiders and bats.

They switched on the lights. A large, scaly lizard examined them thoughtfully. It had no tail. Its long tongue darted out suddenly, in search of some elusive insect. Samir screamed again.

'Calm down, calm down, Samir bhaiyya,' Rahul said soothingly. 'It's a living creature, just like you or me.' He had been examining the lizard just as carefully as it had been examining them, and was wonderstruck to find a new tail, a tender grey appurtenance, emerging from under the stump of the old, discarded one.

'Look, look!' he said. 'New tails for old!'

Frank Sinatra continued playing in the background, and they switched off the lights again.

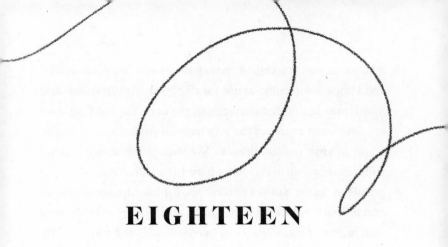

EIGHTEEN

Munni had the rajma-chawal and kadhi ready and packed by 11 a.m. A runner from Women for Peace took the tiffin carrier to Babli Mohan's home. Babli called to thank Shanta. She sounded rested, less stressed than the day before.

Shanta had spent the night in her own flat and returned upstairs early in the morning. Surya was sitting at his mother's feet, trimming her toenails. Visitors were still discouraged, but Ritika and Satish had peeped in, as had Rahul and Samir.

'I want all my children here with me,' Matangi announced suddenly. 'Satish and Ritika, and the boys. You stay right here, Shanta, and Surya too.'

Surya tried to discourage her, but she remained adamant. When they were all gathered around her, she cleared her throat and began speaking. 'I've been very ill,' she said. 'I know that you were all worried that I would die, but it's not time for me to go—not yet. I thought I should tell you, while I'm still alive, and you are all here together, about my will. I have drawn on Satish's help, as he is best qualified to guide on these matters.'

Satish remained expressionless as she continued.

'As you know, I have fixed deposits, assets and debentures worth about 13 crore rupees. I received the seed money many, many decades ago from my uncle Satish, my mother's brother. I added my husband's money, his provident fund, insurance, etc., to this corpus. I saved and invested wisely, and I hope it will come in use for all of you. Surya, Shanta and Satish are already cosignatories in the bank for fixed deposits of about three crores each. You have all got individual flats in C100 in your names already. My youngest grandson Rahul will inherit my flat, this flat where I live, after me. My other grandson Samir will get two crores, for his education, and to find his path, whatever it may be. Rahul will get an additional sum of one crore, when he is twenty-five. Our faithful family members, Munni and Lali, will receive five lakhs each. Twenty lakhs to Shanta's organization, Women for Peace, to support the good work they are doing. The rest will be held in trust by Shanta, who will use it as she thinks fit, taking Surya, Satish and Ritika's suggestions into consideration.'

Her children were listening carefully, not knowing quite how to respond. Shanta darted a curious side-glance at Satish.

'Little Pappoo, who stayed under my roof, will get rupees one lakh, which Lali will hold for him. Shanta will ensure that any further sums required for his well-being and education will be provided to him. And now, the most important instruction.' She began coughing, and Lali rushed to get her a glass of water. She paused and gathered herself together. 'The *most* important instruction. Nothing must be given from my savings to temples or holy men. Nothing.'

That got them smiling. She was as clearheaded as ever.

'I appeal to you, my beloved children, to hold together as a family after I have gone. I have dedicated my life to you and I shall be looking after you long after I die, from wherever I am.'

What could they say? 'You will live for a very long time, Matangi-Ma,' Surya said brokenly, only to be silenced by a dismissive wave of her hand.

'Go away now, go away, dear children,' she said, suddenly tired. Rahul went and kissed her withered hand with the coral ring on her finger. Lali sat down on the floor beside her bed and began weeping.

As a family, they had not been given to drama. Surya, Shanta, Satish—they had all kept their troubles and sorrows to themselves, and their joys had been underplayed as well. Matangi's uncharacteristic announcement left them uneasy and unprepared. It had the sense of an ending.

Surya returned to his notes. The book was becoming more unwieldy every day. There was so much he wanted to say, to record, to remember—such a double-decker full of ideas— but he still lacked the overarching theme that could hold it all together.

He had begun on a new chapter, which he tentatively titled 'Bharat Mata'. There was a print of Rabindranath Tagore's famous painting of Mother India hanging on the wall beside his desk. He had toyed with the idea of using this as the cover illustration for his book. The lyrical wash image depicted a four-armed goddess. In her hands she held prayer beads, a white cloth, a sheaf of rice and a parchment manuscript. This early visual representation of the nationalist idea was now so overlaid with interpretation and mistrust that Surya realized it would be contentious to use it.

Surya looked through his carefully filed notes again. 'Bankim Chandra Chattopadhyay's 1882 novel *Anandmath* conflated the nation and the mother into a single nationalist inspiration. At what point had the ancient matriarchal traditions been overtaken by Savarna patriarchy? Was India patriarchal or matriarchal?'

He put his notes away. He would leave these debates for another day. Meanwhile, C100 continued as a functioning matriarchy, with Matangi Devi as its presiding deity. So she had always been, and so she would remain. Namastasye, Namastasye, Namastasye, Namo Namah.

Riyaz was playing in the empty classroom of the quarantine centre outside his village. He had arrived there with his uncle and aunts and cousin. The long march home had begun as an adventure that had slowly lost its charm. The hungry wait at the railway station, after they had gone through the puris that Lali had packed for them. The crowds, the confusion, the wilting spirits. When the train lurched to a stop at their junction, Riyaz had dived out and turned a joyous somersault.

The bus ride through green fields and rough roads, and then the trek to the quarantine centre. They walked through furrowed paths and fields of ripening sugarcane, still muddy with recent rain. Riyaz saw a snake slither by, right under his feet, and he was afraid and rushed ahead to catch up with his uncle.

The local panchayat had made provisions for the returning travellers. A man in a khaki uniform took their temperatures and recorded their names. The men were to sleep in a large hall, the women and smaller children in two empty classrooms. The desks and benches were lined up against the wall. He had settled before one of the battered desks, pretending to play 'school school', but it was no fun at all in the damp room, with strangers parked on their mattresses, which were laid out in neat lines at a distance from each other.

The villagers were kind, and the food was good, a spicy jhol with rice and a heap of bananas piled on steel thalis. Riyaz had two bananas and went out into the veranda to play his favourite game. He was driving a car. VRROOM VROOM, he went, VROOOM VROOOM.

His cousin Nazneen was playing hopscotch at the other end of the long veranda. She had drawn out the squares and rectangles with a piece of chalk she had found near the abandoned blackboard. The chalk was a pretty pink colour, and she had drawn the lines neat and straight. She threw a flat stone on the cement floor and picked it up; one foot, hop, and then two, and then one foot again. She had just landed with both feet on the next marker when a green snake came sliding swiftly in and skirted her foot.

Nazneen screamed. The snake wrapped itself around her ankle. She screamed again. Riyaz could see her eyes, blank with terror, as she looked towards him. He rushed to help her. His aunt screamed and threw a worn rubber slipper towards her daughter. The snake disentangled itself and returned to the snarl of lantana bushes outside.

Now his aunt was clutching her daughter. His uncle was trying to call somebody from the village to come and help them. The man in the khaki clothes who had taken their temperature had gone home. Everyone was in a panic.

Nazneen had gone stiff with terror. Riyaz could see the two puncture wounds on her ankle. She was sweating, and breathing in uneven gasps. A tall man with a red scarf tied around his mouth stepped forward. He was wearing gold hoops in his ears and a dusty white dhoti. Riyaz noticed all these things about him as he knelt down before Nazneen and took charge of the situation.

'Don't move,' he told her. 'Stay still, or the poison will spread.' He tied a tourniquet around her calves and began sucking at the poison from the snakebite.

Riyaz couldn't even bear to look at the terrible scene. He put his hands over his eyes, but he couldn't help but peep through his fingers. His aunt was weeping loudly. 'Why didn't the snake bite me?' she wailed. 'Tell it to come back, to bite me instead!'

The man told his aunt to be quiet and to hold on to Nazneen's foot. 'Don't let her move,' he said. 'Hold her gently but firmly. And stop making so much noise.'

He stepped out into the overgrown grounds. Was he looking for the snake? Riyaz wondered. But no, he bent down and plucked a plant from the ground. Then he picked up two large stones, one flat and one round, and returned to the veranda. They watched with frightened anticipation as he began grinding the leaves he had plucked between the two stones until they yielded a stringy, milky paste.

Nazneen had been twitching slightly but now she lay still. Riyaz wondered if she was dead. The man began sucking at her foot again. His face turned purple with concentration as his lips made small delicate movements to ease the venom out. He would spit vigorously, then begin sucking again.

Finally, he sat back, exhausted. Riyaz rushed to his aid and put his small arms around the man's back. The man was drenched in sweat. He patted Riyaz as though to thank him, and placed a poultice of green leaf-paste on the wound. He put the rest of the paste in his mouth and let it sit there for a while before he spat it out. He asked for water and Riyaz rushed to get it for him, from the red plastic water bottle Lali had given him when he set out on his journey.

The man poured in the water from Riyaz's bottle carefully into his mouth, gargled it around and spat it out with startling vigour. Then he put the red scarf around his face and told Riyaz to take Nazneen to lie down inside. 'She will sleep for a day and be fine by tomorrow,' he said, and then he went out to the grounds again and sat himself on a low rock. His eyes were closed in prayer and he was muttering something under his breath.

Nazneen didn't eat or drink anything after that. She slept through the night and awoke the next morning as good as new. Riyaz sat up most of the night, terrified that a snake would slither across the floor to bite him. The next morning he went up to the man who had saved Nazneen's life. He introduced himself, and the man told him his name was Pandu.

'I want to learn how to cure a snakebite,' Riyaz said to Pandu. 'I am afraid of snakes; I sat up all night afraid that one would come and bite me.'

Pandu knelt down and held Riyaz's hand. 'The first thing you have to do if you want to cure snakebite is not to be afraid of snakes,' he said, in a man-to-man sort of voice, not as though he were talking to someone a third of his height. They walked around the grounds together. Pandu pointed out some plants, explained that they were secret cures for snakebites, and even told him their names.

'That's kolar sag,' he said. 'The leaf juice can be applied on bites. These pretty-looking plants are shatavari—it's very useful too. I make a juice from it and keep it with me when I go on my travels. We are locked up here for a long time—I will teach you more about plants, not just for snakebites, but for stomach aches, and jaundice, and eye infections, and insect bites that don't heal. But first let me tell you the most important thing about snakebites. Most of the people who die of it die from terror, not poison. They get heart failure from the fear of it, so they die. I'm not sure if the snake that bit the little girl was poisonous. I didn't see it, though you did. So I took all the precautions needed if a poisonous snake had bitten her.'

'It was green,' Riyaz volunteered, 'with black spots on it.'

'Hmmmm,' Pandu replied. He was silent for a while. 'If a snake comes near you, just say "Astik! Astik!". That's the name of the king of the snakes, and they respect anyone who takes his name.'

That night, Riyaz murmured 'Astik! Astik!' to himself before he fell asleep. He dreamt of Matangi, and of the room on the top floor where she lived. She was smiling, and giving him a toffee, and telling him not to be afraid.

Samir packed a few clothes into an overnight bag, donned a face mask, and set out to spend a few days at his friend Neel's farmhouse. He hadn't left home since the lockdown began, and there was a jauntiness to his step and a smile on his face. Surya's driver-cook, Rudra Singh, had returned to work, and was dropping him to Neel's place, in the SUV.

The car took some time to start up. Samir looked around in wonder. The world looked full of possibility again. The June sky was unseasonably cloudy, as a cyclone formation moved up from the west coast. The air was clean and fresh. The city's infamous pollution seemed a distant nightmare. The traffic was building up, but most people were staying home as the pandemic numbers continued to spike.

Rudra Singh wore his mask slung like a bowtie around his neck. He was convinced that the virus was a Chinese plot, and that the Pakistan army had specially bred the locusts only to dispatch them to India to destroy the crops and spread the virus.

How had they emerged unscathed, Samir wondered. The world had seemed to stop in its tracks, and now perhaps it was cautiously veering to a new reality. Not so cautiously, really, with the upsurge of anger and hatred and riots and deaths and disasters everywhere, but C100 had carried on somehow, and survived.

Samir had plans. He would go to Bihar in the coming months, to visit his father's ancestral home. The old house fronted by mango and litchi trees, which he had seen across the many photos his uncle had shared, where the caretaker and his daughter would look after him. Perhaps his friend Neel would join him too. Uncle Aniruddha was fixing all the details. When the world returned to its feet. When.

Samir had received an email from his uncle Aniruddha that morning. 'I hope to see you soon,' it said. 'And to share the joys of litti-chokha with you. But everything is so uncertain just now. I thought I would share this quote from the physicist Carlo Rovelli, on the modern view of physical reality: "We must unlearn our natural instincts, particularly in order to accept reality." I don't know how this translates into a less abstract lesson for daily life, but I'm trying to learn.'

Samir was getting fonder of his uncle, looking forward to visiting Bihar. He had drawn up an itinerary. He would visit the Buddhist sites. He would go to Nalanda, the ancient centre of Buddhist learning, founded in the fifth century, destroyed in 1202. Perhaps he would enrol in the newly founded Nalanda International University, returning to his roots. It seemed a safer bet than the United States, these days. The UK sounded even more confused.

He had been reading about the Buddha. 'The mind is everything. What you think, you become.' And then Samir had found a line from his teachings. 'Imagine all the sands of the Ganges river. Imagine each grain of sand as a world, and within each grain of sand another world.' Or something like that. A bit like the parallel universe NASA had discovered in its cosmic ray detection experiment. Mindboggling.

Samir was not normally over-philosophical, but then, as he told himself, in such times, one was allowed to be.

Matangi had insisted that she wanted to step out of the room. She made her way to the veranda, unaided, clutching at her walker, and stared out at the scene below, the drive, the road, the park across the road, with unseeing eyes.

A young barbet, with a glossy green-brown coat and a comically large beak, flew up from the red cotton tree outside the Sens' house. It began tweeting rhythmically, almost as though it were reciting a poem. Too-hay-too-hay-too-hay-too-hay. Inside the room, the cuckoo clock began chiming almost in unison. A helicopter whirred overhead. Crows cawed in the trees below.

Matangi could sense the bird fluttering around her. 'So you have come back to see me, Mirchi,' she whispered. 'I must learn to fly too. We will fly away together, one of these days.'

EPILOGUE

SAMIR

Those three months of the early lockdown that I spent at C100 were the slowest, gentlest and also the most intense in my life. There were so many things about myself, about my parents, my relationship with Surya, that I had consigned to a vacuum bag labelled 'Convenient Amnesia'. I was afraid to address those questions, terrified of what the answers might be.

How these months have slipped by. It seems a lifetime ago already. All of us living there together, on those four floors. Time played tricks with us in those months—it expanded, contracted, went truant, sometimes even disappeared as a timelessness swept over those quiet days and nights.

I remember how Surya had taken over all the housework on the first floor. He would wake at dawn to sweep and swab and dust and it was all done when I awoke in the mid-morning, wiping the sleep from my eyes. There was always butter and bread and milk and eggs in the fridge, and fruit. He cooked dal and vegetables and rice. Never chapatis—he hadn't mastered those. Munni would bring a stack from downstairs.

My clothes were always washed and ironed. I would see him sometimes, his tall frame bent over the folding ironing board, whistling softly, or just looking thoughtful, as he sorted out my shorts and frayed jeans. I told him not to bother ironing my clothes, but he did. 'I enjoy housework,' he would say, and I would leave it at that.

It's shocking that he is the one that went, that Covid took him first. Those early months, of blue skies and balmy weather, had left us unprepared for what was to happen.

I remember how we would sweep the leaves in the park, with the tall brooms—the brittle yellow neem leaves, the tender buds of nibori with their pungent smell. It all happened so suddenly, the end of that midsummer dream. I had been at my friend Neel's farmhouse when he first took ill. Surya had tested negative that first time, but the fever wouldn't go away. Shanta bua nursed him with fierce love, and he had recovered, got back to work on his book, when one day we found him slumped over his desk.

I don't want to think about what happened after that. I phoned our neighbour, Dr Nambiar, who was on his way to the hospital in full protective gear. He looked tired, worn out and resigned as he felt Surya's pulse. 'Too late,' he said sorrowfully, 'it's too late to do anything now. We are all too late on this.'

I had lost the man who had been my mother, my father, my best friend. I couldn't bear to continue to stay there, after that, on the first floor, with just Dollar and my broken heart for company. Rahul saw me through a lot, he became my big brother.

We went through the tests, all of us, and anxiously awaited the results. We took daily readings on the oximeter, we mourned, we prayed, we tried to somehow rise above the times. When everything seemed clear, I knew it was time for me to leave.

When I decided to drive to Bihar Sharif with the faithful Rudra Singh, to spend time in my biological grandfather's house, I left Dollar with Rahul. His mother didn't make the expected fuss. Ritika aunty was incredibly kind and loving, she and Satish kaka, and I felt for the first time that my father's brother was there for me, all the way.

My uncle, Aniruddha Sharan Jha, was devastated. He hadn't been able to meet his old friend again, after the long silence between them. He had the old house cleaned up and prepared to welcome me, even as Satish kaka sorted out the e-pass, the home quarantine, the paperwork.

Life is what happens to you when you are busy making other plans. So here I am, in Lal Kothi with its high ceilings and red oxide floors. It's like the parallel universes I was obsessed with, when the summer was still innocent

There are grandiosely conceived but amateurishly executed portraits of my grandfather, and his father, with peeling gilt frames. I have chosen a bedroom on the first floor, overlooking the garden. Only yesterday, the chowkidar-chacha, Ram Naresh-ji, told me it had been my father's bedroom too, many, many years ago. Aditya Sharan Jha had slept there, and I liked to imagine that a bit of him continued to reside there. I put up the photo of my mother Samira on the desk, and felt a certain satisfaction that she too was home at last, with her son.

There are geckos on the walls, darting about busily or waiting immobile for their prey, as the mood may strike them. I am no longer afraid of them—they are like sentinels, agile guardians—although I haven't yet developed any affection for them. Tomorrow is another day, although all the days I have spent here have rolled into one seamless succession of moments.

I eat litti-chokha, and ramsalan, and nimona. The other day, Ram Naresh's daughter made me delicious besan laddoos. That reminded me of Matangi-Ma, and I found myself sobbing uncontrollably. I must return to C100 soon, while she is still there.

I think I am in love. Ram Naresh's grandniece, Sukhda, has been staying here for a while. She is incredibly beautiful, and also talented and self-assured. She smells of lichis, and mangoes, and the essence of jasmine.

Sukhda wants to do her MPhil in physics. She is no village belle, and in any case, Bihar Sharif is no village. She is much, much brighter than me, I respect that, and I wish I could introduce her to Surya, that she could meet him.

We bumped into each other, quite literally, in the garden. She was admiring a strange-looking object hanging from the branches of the mango tree. I deduced that it was a nest of some kind.

'Is that a weaverbird's nest, or a tailorbird's?' she asked me.

I confessed I didn't know.

'I think it's a tailorbird,' she said contemplatively. 'They make their nests with these long leaves, while weaverbirds use only dry twigs and straw.'

She began walking off in the other direction. I was desperate to continue the conversation. Just then, I heard a familiar sound from high above the branches. Too-hay, too-hay, too-hay, too-hay.

I stopped her. 'Listen, Sukhda,' I said. 'Just listen. That's a barbet singing. I saved a barbet's life once—and helped nurse it back until it could fly again. Then we set it free.'

'Really?' she said, all wide-eyed, and I could see that I had caught her attention. I told her about Matangi-Ma, and how she had sent me in search of the abandoned barbet, and about all my family in C100.

Just then, the barbet descended to a branch almost eye-level with us and began again on its peculiar song. I could see its big, awkward beak, its sharp, curious eyes, and I felt that I had encountered an old friend, and that it was singing for us, for me and Sukhda. We became friends after that—I guess she decided I wasn't just a spoilt city boy.

We inhabit a different sort of timelessness here. I keep track of what's happening in the world outside. The pandemic retreats, then rears its head again. It has disoriented me, leaving me stronger in some things, anxious and afraid in others.

I speak to Rahul every other day. He keeps me abreast of what's happening in C100 and its precincts. The Sens are selling their house and planning to move into an expensive under-construction care-home in Dehra Dun. They have rented an apartment for the meantime. The builder will be converting their house into a block of flats—although nobody is really buying in this depressed economy, only selling.

Rahul's second exciting item of news is about Shanta's cat, Miss Trump. She had a litter around the time Surya had first fallen ill. The black bully-cat who lived in the garden next door and was probably the father, had made his way indoors and killed one of the kittens. Rahul informed me that the rest of the litter was doing well, and that Shanta had gifted two of them to the policewoman, Babli Mohan, who seems to have become her new best friend. Dollar is fine too—Rahul is watching out for monsoon ticks.

Rudra Singh is here with me. He hasn't got over our loss. I have seen him burst into tears at the mention of Surya's name. But he appreciates this house, the grounds, the ornate facade, the long veranda. Rudra Singh is from Garhwal, but I can see that his scorn of Bihar and things Bihari has been mitigated by this encounter.

He cooked for me last evening, a special chicken curry bathed in garlic. I am eating better than I ever did in hostel, or even C100. I am sleeping well too, in this fragile bubble so removed from the woes of the world. The earthquakes in Delhi. The cyclones. The floods. The cross-border firing with Pakistan. Chinese incursions into Ladakh. It's an endless litany of woes, with that cunning virus at the heart of it, as it morphs and mutates on its sinister path. I'm told it's tiring out, losing its sting.

I called Lali to ask her about Pappoo. She forwarded a video in which he was doing a version of a Michael Jackson moonwalk, while mouthing the words of some unintelligible song, to a 'Billie Jean' rhythm. He looked happy, and his footwork was simply fantastic. I sent Lali an emoji with two hearts and she sent back a photo of Matangi-Ma, standing in the veranda, wearing a mask. She stood as upright as ever. The expression on her face was inscrutable under the mask.

I remember her words when I was leaving, when I had gone up to get her blessings before we drove off. My heart was heavy with all the unsaid things I didn't know how to share with her. She was wearing a mask and I was, too—we had all become more careful by then. She made me sit next to her, like old times, and stroked my face, as though she was trying to read it for one last time.

'Stop grieving,' she said. 'It will hurt him. He has to look forward in his new journey, not turn back at every step, worrying about you.'

That made sense. I wanted Surya to be free and joyous, wherever he was.

'The dead are dead . . .' she continued. 'Life is for the living. We must heal the living, they hurt more than those that have gone.'

She was silent for a while. 'My Suryaveer was a good boy,' she said at last. 'The best of the best. I will catch up with him soon, and he can read me some poetry again. But I'm in no hurry to go, Samir. I have to be here, to look after all of you, don't I?'

She stroked my hair, pulling it back from my face. 'You will get married soon,' she said. 'And then you will bring your bride home. I have a special piece of jewellery I have saved for her—Shanta knows about it.'

I had doubled over with laughter. 'Married!' I had giggled, tears of mirth in my eyes. 'Married! I don't even have a girlfriend yet!' But a part of me took note of her words. She had a way of knowing things . . . as though she could sense the footsteps of future time.

My grandmother is the bravest person I know. She has the courage of a soldier, the fortitude of a saint. She held us all together, in those days, after we found Surya slouched over his desk.

She did not weep when she heard the news. She composed her face into an expressionless mask. 'I want to go down and be with him,' she said.

Rahul got her a visor and gloves. Satish kaka and I led her down the stairs to the first floor. She refused to let us carry her down. We went very slowly, but she was visibly tired by the time we got there.

We had laid Surya out on the floor. Shanta had plucked some flowers from her garden, and scattered them around his feet. His long, bony feet, his tall frame, his familiar blue shorts and white tee shirt. It was unbelievable, a story that had strayed in from some other dimension. It was when Matangi-Ma had settled herself on the floor beside him that the truth of it hit home. Surya had left us. He had gone

She told us to leave. The others did as they were told, all except me and Munni. I sat down beside her. Matangi-Ma knew I was there but she didn't say anything. She was wearing gloves and a visor, but Shanta had told her not to touch him.

How could she not? She stroked his forehead, his cheeks, held his hand. Then she indicated to me that she wanted to go. Munni helped Matangi-Ma up and started sobbing and wailing. Satish insisted on carrying her up, and then Lali wiped her with sanitizer and led her for a bath.

I took her temperature after that and checked her oxygen levels with an oximeter. She seemed to be doing all right. She didn't speak for a week after that, not a word. When I went up to say goodbye, she was her old self again—her skin glowing with inner light, her hair gleaming from the L'Oréal Silver shampoo I had ordered for her on Amazon, in those days from another zone, another time.

Only Satish kaka and I were allowed to be at the funeral. We wore hazmat suits, strange and stifling gear that made me imagine that we had died too and were being dispatched to some dystopian netherworld.

There was a priest in a hazmat suit who said a prayer as we lowered him into the motorized trolley at the electric crematorium. Somebody pressed a button and he was wheeled into the glowing heart of the furnace.

'Goodbye, Surya,' I whispered as I held on to Satish kaka.

I was numb for days. Ritika insisted that I sleep upstairs in their flat, but I resisted. I belonged here, in the home that Surya and I built together. Rahul slept downstairs with me, in my room. Shanta insisted that she would sleep there too, and laid out a mattress in Surya's room.

The containment process had become even stricter. Nobody knew what was happening, but we carried on, somehow, protecting Matangi-Ma in whatever way we could, physically and emotionally. She was the flame of our souls. She held our lives in the palm of her frail hands—even though Surya had slipped through to make his way to strange new lands.

I returned to my room today to find a vase of red and yellow canna flowers placed on the desk that must once have been my father's. I think it's Sukhda who put them there.

I look at the flowers. A barbet is singing somewhere in the garden outside. It sounds familiar and comforting. Sukhda slides into the room, and a whiff of fragrant rain-filled breeze follows her in her wake, from the wet veranda.

She sits down in a chair by the open window, shaking the rain from her hair. The barbet is relentless in its call. 'Do you know what the bird is telling you?' she asks.

I nod stupidly, dumbstruck by her beauty. 'I don't know,' I say. 'I don't know what the bird is telling me. Too-hay, too-hay, too-hay. You explain what that means, since you clearly understand the language of birds.'

'That's not what it's saying,' she replies. 'It is speaking in another language. Bata-de, bata-de, bata-de—that's what it is telling you.'

I listen carefully. Perhaps she is right. Perhaps that is what it's warbling today.

'Bata-de, bata-de!' she continues. 'Tell-me, tell-me! That's what it is saying. Birds speak in Bihari here in Bihar Sharif, not in English! "Tell me your story", it's saying.'

I smile at her. She smiles back. 'I will tell you my story,' I say. 'I'll tell you all my stories, if you will listen to them.'

Something passes between us, silent and powerful. We listen to the clicking sounds of the geckos as they skitter across the wall. She steps out of the room, leaving the door open behind her.

I must return to C100, to sort out Surya's papers, his desk, his memories. I know that I will come back here to Lal Kothi again, and that this too is my home. I will return, I will remain, I will hold all my multiple worlds together.

Bata-de, bata-de, the barbet continues with its song.

SAMIR

I had thought that the story would end with the barbets and the old house in Bihar Sharif, so redolent with memories, but of course it couldn't. That interlude in Lal Kothi seemed textured like a grainy film, like Bihari noir before the gunshots began.

I'm back here, at C100, where everything is the same, and yet it's not. It is now that I feel the sense of an ending, after that cursed yet enchanted year is behind us.

Sukhda has begun coaching classes in Kota. She is determined to make it to the Civil Services. And she will. She will.

It is the month of March. The neem trees are shedding their leaves. They are piling up on the road outside, with no one to sweep them away. I picked up a broom one afternoon and set about cleaning them, and I waited for Suryaveer to join me. That last year, when we had all lived together in lockdown, had been a gift—from time? of time?

I sat down on a bench and wept until I was cleaned out and hollow before I began on the leaves again. The swishing rhythm of the tall broom, the whisper of the neem leaves, all felt charged and hypnotic, as if I had been smoking up. Then it was time for the next online class, and I returned to the house, which seemed emptier than ever.

Ritika had got a job offer in Mumbai and they had decided to give it a try and make the move. It was the sort of job offer one didn't pass up, especially in these hard times. Rahul has got admission in Greenlawns High School, which was where Karan Johar had once studied. Ritika has a flat in Prabhadevi with a sea view.

Satish kaka spends a lot of time in Mumbai now. He too is exploring new opportunities. Rahul told me that his parents are thinking of getting him admitted to a boarding school in

Panchgani. 'Karan Johar studied there as well,' he told me importantly.

I miss Rahul, I really do, every time I pass the second floor. It remains locked up most days, and there's often a pile of mail outside. The postman must leave the mail in the postbox on the ground floor, but I'm not sure how it gets up there.

I spend more time with Matangi-Ma, to make up for Rahul not being here. She has grown mysteriously sharper, even more alert than before. We listen to the news on television, about the virus and the vaccine. She clutches her embroidered handkerchief and asks me questions. What was Bihar Sharif like? Do I want to go to America? What do I plan to do with my life?

I don't know what I want to do with my life. Nothing seems certain any more. I feel as though we are lost in a video-game simulation, like the ones Rahul used to love. I try to explain this to Matangi-Ma, but I don't have the words.

One afternoon I did a strange thing. I took a clock that hung in our flat and dismembered it. It's strange that I still call it our flat—it's just my flat now. I took the clock and prised out its hands—the long hand and the minute hand and then the seconds hand. I opened up the battery compartment and threw the batteries out. Then I hung it back on the wall. Now what was that supposed to mean?

I took Matangi-Ma for her vaccine shot. Lali and I carried her down—she was almost weightless, like a large bird. We went with Rudra Singh, who still comes over when I need him. Shanta couldn't make it; she wasn't feeling well, she said, which was unlike her.

Matangi-Ma seemed to enjoy the drive to the hospital. She chatted with Lali and Rudra Singh. I had made arrangements for a wheelchair at the gate, and we made it to a large atrium where rows and rows of people were seated patiently in plastic bucket chairs, awaiting their turn. India is a young country, with more than 50 per cent of its population under the age of twenty-five. I am one of them. The average age of an Indian is twenty-nine years. But there, in the vaccination hall, there were more elderly people than I had ever collectively encountered before. They seemed to be in high spirits, laughing and chattering and sharing biscuits with each other. There was a separate counter for wheelchairs and we were done in fifty minutes, including the half-hour wait after the jab.

It had been a cheerful excursion, with a picnic feel to it. She didn't seem to be having any negative reactions. I left her in her room with Lali. I moped around in the first-floor flat, feeling hemmed in. Nobody was sure when my college would open up again. Online classes kept me going, but only just. I would remain parked here, with Matangi-Ma and Shanta, until I got back to college. There was time enough to figure things out after that.

That was when Shanta threw a thunderbolt my way. 'I am moving to the hills,' she said. 'I have found the perfect place, in Ranikhet. I'm relocating there this May. We have all to follow our dreams—it's our duty to ourselves. I've done my duty by everybody all my life, it's my chance now.'

I couldn't believe my ears. She couldn't move—she couldn't abandon C100 along with all the others. 'What about Matangi-Ma?' I asked with panic in my voice. 'Who will look after her? She can't live here alone! And I have to return to college!'

'I will take her with me,' Shanta said calmly. 'This isn't over yet, this pandemic. There will be a second surge, and a third, maybe a fourth. These politicians are deluded, and the doctors are in denial too. It's best to leave this city, while we can.'

'I've discussed it with Matangi-Ma,' she continued, 'and she approves of the idea. Lali will come with us. Munni will join us later—she plans to spend time with her grandchildren before that. It will be beautiful up there, with the mountains and the flowers and the pine trees and the deodars.'

'She can't see the landscape,' I pointed out. 'She is blind. Let's face it, she is too old to make the move. And it will be too cold for her.'

Shanta bua was not fazed. 'We will do the journey in two stages, with a night break in Rampur or Ramnagar, depending on which road we take. And we will come back here in mid-November, even though it's warm and sunny in the mountains in winter, except at night. We will return for the winter months. Perhaps you will come and stay with us in the summer months.'

My world was falling apart. Shanta couldn't cart my grandmother around like a sack of potatoes. 'I have discussed it with Matangi-Ma,' she said, unrelenting. Mummy will have her second dose up in the hills. She thinks it is an adventure—she is excited.'

'What about Trump?' I said desperately. 'And Dollar? What about them?'

She fell silent for a moment. 'I'm still reaching a decision on that,' she said. 'Cats don't like to change houses. It would upset her. And Dollar—I would like to see how he adjusts. There are leopards there sometimes, I'm told.'

That was it. I screamed out loud and shook her by the shoulders. 'You want my grandmother to be eaten up by leopards?'

'The kukuriya-baghs—they eat dogs sometimes, never humans.' She didn't seem shaken, although I had physically shaken her up a minute ago.

'I'm sorry, Shanta bua,' I said. 'I'm very confused. This doesn't seem like such a good idea.'

'It's now or never,' she said. 'There comes a time when one must follow one's dreams.' There was a note of urgency in her voice.

The Blind Matriarch

I saw the point of that, somewhat, but it seemed an impractical, even impossible idea.

'I'm going out with my friends,' I said, 'to have a drink.' It seemed the only thing to do in the circumstances. None of my few and scattered friends were free, and I wound up with an old schoolfellow who lived down the road, having beer in the flat. At home. At C100.

That was the night Matangi-Ma fell down the stairs. I was turning of the light, after putting the glasses in the kitchen. It had been soothing to be with somebody my own age, even though we didn't have much to say to each other. I had found an apple in the fridge and was about to bite into it when I heard a sound outside.

I peeped out cautiously. Perhaps it was a burglar trying to break into the second floor. Then I heard the whimpering. I put on the stairwell light and crept upstairs. She was lying there on the second-floor landing, curled up like a kitten.

I picked her up and carried her back upstairs. She had wet herself when she fell, and her kaftan was damp. The door was ajar. There was nobody in the room.

'I am not hurt,' she said, in a voice that was strangely normal. 'I haven't broken anything.'

I laid her tenderly on the bed and called for Lali. She had just gone to the bathroom, she said. Matangi-Ma had never tried to leave the room before, ever. What had gone wrong with her today?

'I was looking for them,' Matangi-Ma said. 'I was looking for them.'

I wanted to burst into tears but I controlled myself. Lali cleaned her up and changed her clothes. I stood in the balcony and waited. I could smell the night flowers. When I went inside, there was the scent of incense. Lali had lit an agarbatti.

'I will sleep here tonight,' I said. 'Lay out a mattress on the floor, please.'

Lali protested that I go back, that they would be fine, but I insisted. 'I want to stay with my grandmother tonight,' I insisted. She laid out a mattress. I crept down to lock the first-floor flat and returned to that beloved, familiar room.

I woke up the next morning with a sense of immense clarity, with no sign of the hangover that might have dogged me. I called Shanta and told her what had happened. Dr Nambiar made a house visit and declared she was none the worse for wear. Shanta was in touch with a doctor she knew about a portable X-ray. I helped Matangi-Ma as she made her way to the balcony. She breathed in the morning air and looked sightlessly at the light of the new day. She was smiling and seemed deeply content, as though she knew something, as though she had been told something.

It was time to let go. 'I will come with you to the hills,' I said to Shanta. 'I will settle you both in. Matangi-Ma will enjoy the change, and the mountain air will be good for her.'

She looked uncertain. 'I'm not so sure about our plan any more,' she said.

'The two of you would be alone in this big empty house,' I said. 'Follow your dreams.'

We left it at that. Satish kaka would surely have an opinion as well. There was still the second dose of the vaccine waiting. It would all roll out, in its own time, its own way.

'Samir,' Shanta said, ruffling my hair. 'What would we have done without you, Samir, if you hadn't found her last night?'

My name. Samir. It means the breeze. That's what I felt like then—a morning breeze, a spring breeze. A breeze is not a wind. It has movement. It doesn't occupy any space.

I thought of my mother, of Samira Susan. I could feel her ruffling my hair. I felt good.

The Blind Matriarch

SHANTA

I had always dreamt of living somewhere in the mountains. When my friend and colleague Archana decided, at the age of sixty-eight, to marry her long-time boyfriend, she asked me to take over her home in Ranikhet.

'It's a beautiful house; I've built it brick by brick, log by log,' she said. 'My fiance Andy—Avdhesh Patel, but he calls himself Andy—is from Fiji but now American. This will help us get over our various visa hassles, and he can get an OCI card.'

Archana's words gave me courage. If she could begin life again in her sixties, I could too.

I knew her house, it overlooked the Sat Tal lake and was breathtakingly pretty. 'You could use it as a holiday home,' she said. 'Women for Peace have a branch in Mukteswar—you could keep an eye on the work they are doing, with livelihoods and sustainable agriculture.'

I made a spot decision. 'I'll move there,' I told her. 'I will live there with my mother.' I had already seen it coming, I knew what was in store.

We made the move here, to Pine Cottage, before the second wave of the pandemic hit. Trump and Dollar, and Lali, and Matangi-Ma. Samir came with us and helped us settle in. Lali was both afraid of and enchanted by these new surroundings. The chowkidar's wife taught her how to knit. My mother inhaled the scent of flowers, listened to the whispering breeze, and smiled. Dollar wore a smart spiked collar to protect him from prowling leopards, and spent most of his day dozing under the dining table. Cats are supposed to resist change, but Trump took to the new surroundings—we would find her purring with contentment in my new study.

We had challenges. The forest fires were terrifying. Sometimes we had to shut the windows to keep the ash-laden breeze out until the wind changed.

Last night—was it just last night?—Dollar was agitated. I heard him scratching at my bedroom door and let him in. I had left the louvred window in the corridor open. There was a smell outside, a fetid smell, and a strange sound, like a saw grating wood. A bagh, a leopard, was on the prowl outside.

I let Dollar in. He crawled under my bed. Then I went to check on Matangi-Ma. The night lamp cast a gentle orange light. She was curled up to one side. An owl hooted outside.

I reached out to hold her hand, to check on her. Her eyes were open, all-seeing. She had left her body, she had gone.

I sat beside her for a long time. A dreamlike memory arose, of a young Matangi-Ma before she had lost her sight, playing badminton. She had been barefoot; she had kicked off her sandals. Her face was flushed with excitement, the pallav of her sari fastened around her waist.

Lali woke up to find me there. Dawn was breaking across the pine-crested hills. I didn't have to tell her, to say anything. She understood. She closed Matangi-Ma's eyes gently shut. She stroked her forehead. She knelt down and prayed. She wept.

She opened the windows and the morning breeze spilled into the room. I phoned Satish and Ritika. I spoke to Rahul. I told Samir.

They could not come for the funeral. The country was in collapse. Delhi and Mumbai were in lockdown. Samir set up a call where we could say our goodbyes.

It was the first of May. May Day. The project head at the Mukteshwar branch of Women for Peace, a local Pahadi, helped make arrangements for the funeral. Our chowkidar Man Singh and three young men from the village carried the bier to the secluded burning ground beside the Nal-Damayanti Lake. I lit the pyre. The flames were small, almost playful, until they gathered momentum. The pinewood smelt sweet, and the haze from the flames made the hillside shimmer.

In the plains below, thousands of pyres were burning. There were bodies waiting for wood, for fire, for a patch of land to bury them. The young were dying, old men and women were dying, children were dying.

Matangi-Ma had gone. She was not there to protect us. We were on our own.

We had been a family, once. India had been a nation. It wasn't just a virus that was destroying us, it was the demon seed that we had spawned. The summer of 2021. Vikram Samvat 2078—the Hindu calendar had deemed it 'Rakshasa'—the year of the demon.

I lit an earthen lamp and placed it on the floor by Matangi-Ma's bed. Her room was just as it had been, the bed unmade. I folded her quilt and smoothed out her pillow. Her embroidered handkerchief was still lying there, crumpled up as though she had only just held it.

Vikram Samvat 2078. It was the end of an era. The end of an epoch.

RAHUL

I dream of death a lot these days. I see him in the daytime too—
always a he, never a she. He came to take Matangi-Ma, from
far, far away, high in the hills, though she did not die of
Covid. He took our physical training teacher, Khosla Sir,
last week. We had an online condolence meeting where the
principal and some teachers paid tribute to him. I hadn't
met Khosla Sir properly at school, as it had been mostly
online after I joined, and when we had physical lessons
before the second lockdown, physical training classes had
been suspended. RIP, Khosla Sir.

Death looks like a cross between Yama, the Lord of
Death from the *Amar Chitra Katha* comics, and Thanos,
the intergalactic warlord from *Avengers: Endgame*. I am not
afraid of him. But I am angry that he took my Matangi-Ma.

My father is in an ICU ward. He was diagnosed positive
for Covid the day Matangi-Ma left for what Mummy said was
her eternal abode. His oxygen levels had fallen dangerously,
but things seem better now. At least he has a hospital bed
and an uninterrupted supply of oxygen. It's not like that in
Delhi. I read that people, even children, are dying when the
oxygen supply dries up, and that the government is doing
nothing about it.

I have begun to practise deep breathing to build up
my lung capacity, but sometimes I find myself suddenly
breathless. Like yesterday. My mother told me it was a
panic attack and that I should breathe slowly in and out and
think of happy things.

I thought of C100 and all the fun we used to have there—
of Dollar and Trump and Samir dada. And Matangi-Ma.
I called Samir dada on WhatsApp and told him about my
panic attack.

'That's normal!' he replied. 'I had one too, yesterday. I didn't know how to handle it, so I went to C100 and played the drums for an hour.'

'Aren't you staying in C100?' I asked.

'I won't be able to stay there alone,' he replied, 'with all of you gone. My college has shut down again, and I'm staying with my friend Dhruv.'

'What's C100 like these days?' I asked.

He was quiet for a while. 'Well, it's lonely and it's dusty and it's full of cobwebs,' he said. 'Shanta bua's garden is a jungle, but there are flowers blooming among the weeds. The barbet is singing on the cotton-silk tree. The Sens' house has been knocked down, but nothing has been built in its place.'

'Did you sense Matangi-Ma's ghost there?' I asked.

Samir dada laughed. 'I don't believe in ghosts—not really—and neither did Matangi-Ma. But I plucked some flowers from amidst the weeds and went up to her room. It was quiet and tidy, as though somebody had cleaned it up—not like the rest of the house. I felt as though she was sitting there, giving me her love.'

'I hope my papa doesn't die and become a ghost,' I said, and began crying loudly, like a baby.

'Let's sing a song together,' Samir dada said, 'the one we used to sing before. Just wait a minute, hold on . . .' He began humming something I couldn't recognize, then put on some music from somewhere, maybe his laptop.

It was the Frank Sinatra song we had sung along to in C100 during the lockdown—'*I did it my way*'.

Then I heard my mother calling me for dinner and I had to rush. The maid has Covid and Mummy is not a great cook. It was dal and bread again, but I didn't complain.

That night I dreamt of death again. He had come for me on a speeding motorcycle, carrying an empty oxygen cylinder. I woke up sweating and told myself not to panic.

Then I had a glass of water and crept into my mother's room. I crawled into bed with her and she held me tight. Real tight.

My mother had told me that Matangi-Ma had gone to her eternal rest. I don't believe that. My grandmother would never want to be away from us. She will come back, someday, somehow, to be with us again.

AGASTYA SEN

The Sens died, in two different hospitals, at almost exactly the same moment. Agastya Sen was in hospital for thirteen days. He had a pulmonary infection, and the black fungus had ravaged his brains. A junior colleague from the Indian Foreign Service kept vigil over him, staying in touch with the doctors at the ICU, ensuring that he received medicines even though the hospitals had run out of life-saving drugs, seeing that his oxygen levels were somehow maintained even as Delhi ran out of the vital lifeline of an uninterrupted oxygen supply. He reached out to a serving officer with connections to find a slot in an overflowing crematorium for the last rites.

He too was a devoted Sanskrit scholar, which explained his loyalty and affection to his former boss. As he returned home, drained and exhausted, after Agastya Sen had been taken to be incinerated to a distant corner of the dusty parking lot that was now a makeshift burning ground, he remembered a line from the Bhagavad Gita. The line that Oppenheimer had quoted after the first atomic bomb was successfully detonated on 16 July 1945.

Kalo-asmi lokakshya-krita-pravruddho

'Now I am become death, the destroyer of worlds.'

ANNA SEN

Anna Sen died the same afternoon, in the parking lot of another hospital, as a neighbour who was part of a volunteer group tried to wheel her into the emergency ward. She was completely dehydrated and delirious.

It was the month of May. The temperature stood at forty-one degrees Celsius. She was declared dead on arrival, and heaped into an ambulance that also served as a hearse. Anna Sen was not given a Christian burial. No one knew or cared who she was. She was consigned to the glowering flames of a mass burial alongside a pile of strangers who had also lost the battle.

'Now I am become death, the destroyer of worlds.'

SHANTA

India has reported 400,000 Covid cases for three days now. I feel as though this is a dispatch from the trenches, even though Kumaon is still relatively safer than Mumbai, Delhi, or Uttar Pradesh. Forty dead bodies were discovered floating in the muddy waters of the Yamuna river. Earlier, there were similar ghastly sightings in Hamirpur, where the Yamuna was awash with rotting carcasses. A hundred decomposing bodies travelling downstream in the Ganga river in Buxar, Bihar. The local administrations dissociated themselves from all these occurrences, saying they were from the neighbouring state of Uttar Pradesh. The sacred Ganga is now the river of death. The authorities have spread nets across the banks to catch the bodies.

I received a phone call today from a stranger to inform me that Anna Sen was dead. Her neighbours had tried to get her to the hospital but too late—there had been no hospital rooms anyway. Anna had been carrying a handbag with a five-hundred-rupee note and a scribbled chit of paper that said 'IN CASE OF EMERGENCY CONTACT SHANTA' with my mobile number.

I said a prayer for Anna and for all of us. My prayers had begun to dry up, to become screams, or sobs, or nightmare rhymes. I cuddled Trump and took comfort in her purring. I put on *Mr India* for Lali to watch. I made myself a cup of tea. I took Dollar for a walk.

The pine leaves crunched underfoot. A yellow monarch butterfly settled on Dollar's snout, then fluttered off. Suddenly there were butterflies everywhere—a multitude of them.

Dollar was pulling me uphill but it was time for us to return home. Suryaveer's SUV was parked outside the house. Samir had sprung a surprise. He was settled in Matangi-Ma's room, chatting with Lali. He was wearing a striped mask. We broke the rules and hugged each other. We wept.

'I had to come up,' he told me. 'I have nobody else now, really. I got engaged yesterday—on Zoom. To Sukhda. Life is too uncertain to wait any longer. We will get married properly later, in Lal Kothi, with my grandparents watching over us. You will officiate over the wedding, Shanta bua. Sukhda will wear the jewellery Matangi-Ma left for her. We will come to Pine Cottage for our honeymoon, and you will be the beloved grandmother of our children, as we add to the population of Bihar.'

An unfamiliar emotion ran through me, like a tremor. I was smiling, I was weeping. Samir—married? He was far too young! But then, these were strange times . . . we had to make our choices while we could. I thought of my brother Suryaveer, and for a brief moment, I became him. Samir would continue the story of our lives, as would Rahul—the story that had been interrupted by the demon year, by the Rakshasa Samvat.

We had egg curry for dinner and Alphonso mangoes from the crate that Samir had brought with him. Then we sat out on the small porch, looking at the stars. A swarm of fireflies hovered over the edge of the garden. Summer lightning flashed in the sky, followed by the sound of distant thunder.

'I'm only here for a night, Shanta bua,' Samir said. 'My friend Dhruv's brother is coming to pick me up tomorrow. We are going for a trek, high up in the mountains.'

'A trek? Why now?' I asked, concerned. But I knew what was driving him.

'There are some things a man must do, alone, before he gets married,' Samir replied. 'I want to go as high as I can, to see things from afar—this country, this planet, the night sky . . .'

'This country . . .' I said reflectively. 'Mother India.' I choked up with tears—not of sorrow, not of joy, just exhaustion and anxiety and despair.

Samir ignored my tears. He bent down and kissed my hand.

'Mother India.' he said. 'Mother India. You remember that poem that Surya was so fond of? By Walt Whitman?'

He recited the lines softly, as though to himself.

'The past and present wilt—I have fill'd them, emptied them,
And proceed to fill my next fold of the future.'

I remembered the lines too, and Surya's gravelly voice. 'I contain multitudes,' I whispered. 'I am large—I contain multitudes.'

ACKNOWLEDGEMENTS

To the barbet who was our guest at home for a week. To the Indian Joint Family. To films, television serials and web-series about the Indian Joint Family.

Ambrish Satvik opened my eyes to inconsistencies and lazy vision. Pragya Tiwari helped me focus on the larger picture.

Special gratitude to Pratishtha Singh, Anu Singh, Neeta Gupta, Juliette Frustié, and all those who believed in this book. Thank you Sukhman Khera for your insights and unflagging support.

Thank you Jon Curzon and Artellus Ltd. Gratitude to my editor Manasi Subramaniam for so many things. Shubhi Surana and all the rest of the Penguin Random House team, thank you for your patience and constant cooperation. Gunjan Ahlawat for that beauty of a cover. Lavanya Asthana for bringing it to life with needle and thread.